d!"

yell   he

mig   n as

it h

en-

tion

she

wou

the

trig   but

the   ed

into   ard

her   had

stru   the

sour

ed.

MOMENT OF TRUTH

"Go away!" he yelled. "You're dead! You're dead!"

Jink, the outlaw, was trying to aim the pistol as he had. Jonathan was afraid to shoot him, afraid he might hit Ellie. His aim was by no means as certain as it had once been.

He tried yelling to distract Jink, but Jink's attention was now riveted on Ellie.

"Shoot him, Ellie," Jonathan said, hoping that she could do it before it was too late. "Do it now."

Ellie heard him, and her finger tightened on the trigger. She didn't think she would be able to do it, but the thought of how Burt looked in his coffin flashed through her head, and she remembered exactly how his head had hit the bed of the wagon when Jink had struck her. She remembered with sudden clarity the sound it had made.

The hammers of the shotgun were already cocked.

She pulled the trigger.

OUTRAGE
AT BLANCO

❉◆❉

BILL CRIDER

A DELL BOOK

Published by
Dell Publishing
a division of
Bantam Doubleday Dell Publishing Group, Inc.
1540 Broadway
New York, New York 10036

ISBN: 0-440-23454-9

Printed in the United States of America

Published simultaneously in Canada

January 1999

10 9 8 7 6 5 4 3 2 1

OPM

This one is for James Reasoner:
Masked Writer of the Plains

Chapter 1

———— ❦ ————

Jink Howard sat in the shade of a tree and ate tomatoes out of a can while Ben Atticks raped the woman in the wagon bed.

Jink was pretty damn mad because the woman hadn't had anything to open the can with and he'd had to use his own knife. Besides that, he'd ripped open a ragged strip on the middle finger of his left hand on the jagged edge of the can lid, and it was still hurting him.

He heard Ben grunting away like a stud horse, and the wagon was bouncing a little on its springs. The springs squeaked, but the woman didn't make a sound.

"Hurry up, Ben, goddammit," Jink said. "You gonna take all day?"

Ben didn't answer, but soon there was a grunt a bit louder than all the others and then the wagon stopped bouncing.

Jink finished the last tomato, drank the liquid

from the can, and threw it on the ground. As he licked the last drops of liquid off his fingers, he looked at the wagon and saw Ben standing up, pulling on his pants. He'd never taken off his hat.

Ben had his back to the woman, but Jink saw her sit up.

"Look out, Ben," he said.

Ben was a big man, and he turned slowly, like he did most things. The woman was up on her knees, and it looked as if she were about to try pushing him out of the wagon.

Ben leaned down and slapped her with his open hand. The hand didn't seem to be moving fast, but when it struck the side of the woman's face there was a popping sound as loud as a rifle shot.

The woman fell back in the wagon bed out of Jink's sight, but he heard her head when it hit the floorboards with a hollow thud.

Ben straightened up, buckled his belt, walked to the back of the wagon and jumped down, landing heavily and stumbling a little.

"Feisty bitch, ain't she," he said. He ran his fingers through his matted black beard. "You want any of it?"

Jink stood up. He was slim as a snake, narrow in all the places Ben was wide, and short where Ben was tall. He had a bristly three-day growth of brownish whiskers and small, black, snaky eyes that were hard to see under the bony ridge of his brows.

"Damn right I want a little of it," he said. "I thought you wasn't ever gonna finish, though."

"Well, get after it, then," Ben said. He turned back to the wagon. "You reckon she's got any more of them tomatoes in there?"

He rummaged around though the supplies that were scattered in the wagon bed and came up with a can. He held it up and looked at it.

"What'm I supposed to open this with?" he said.

"Use your damn knife," Jink said.

He climbed up in the wagon and looked down at the woman. She had a long, horsey face, with wide, staring blue eyes, and the kind of blond hair that was almost brown. There was blood on her mouth because she had bitten almost through her lower lip, and the whole right side of her face was a red blotch where Ben had slapped her.

Jink dropped his pants and lowered himself on her. "Ain't much to look at, is she?" he said.

The woman twisted to her right and grabbed Jink's injured hand. She bit hard into the finger that he'd cut, mixing her saliva and blood with the blood that was running from the gash.

Jink yowled and grabbed her hair, yanking her head back. The skin of his finger ripped away.

Jink slammed the woman's head against wagon bed. It hit much harder than it had when Ben had slapped her. She was stunned, but that wasn't enough for Jink. He sat back and slugged her on the point of the chin with his fist, and her eyes rolled up in her head.

"Legs ain't bad, though," Ben said, his mouth full

of tomatoes. He'd been too busy opening the can to be bothered with Jink's troubles.

"Yeah," Jink said. "But she's might feisty. You didn't do much to tame her down."

Blood and saliva dripped from his hand onto the wagon bed. He started to wipe his hand on his shirt and then thought better of it. He wiped it on the woman's dress instead.

Then he had another look at the woman. Ben was right about her legs. They were slim and tapered to slender ankles. Her hips were wide, but not too wide, a whole sight prettier than her face. Jink thought he had seen better lookers in most of the whorehouses he'd visited, and the women in the whorehouses weren't anything to brag about. He pulled her dress up over her head so he wouldn't have to look at it. Then he forced himself into her.

It was too bad he'd had to cold-cock her; he would have preferred a little more life in her, maybe a little bit of a struggle, but what the hell. He'd had more than one whore who hadn't had any more spirit to her than a dead woman. He didn't require much of a response. Soon he was grunting as loudly as Ben had.

Listening, Ben smiled behind his beard as he ate the canned tomatoes.

Ellie Taine woke up lying on the hard boards of the wagon bed. At first she thought it had gotten dark, but then she realized that her dress was pulled over her face. Her head was throbbing, and there was a burning between her legs. She reached to touch herself there, and then she remembered what had happened.

She frantically pulled her dress away from her face and sat up suddenly, putting her hands on the sides of her head as if to hold it in place. She sat like that for a minute, starting down at the blood between her legs, at the ripped underclothing that she had sewed herself and that had been torn away from her by the two men.

The men.

They had met the wagon as she was returning from her weekly trip to Rogers' Mercantile with the groceries for her and her husband. They had hailed her, and she had stopped the wagon. There didn't seem to be any harm in that, not so close to town, so close to home.

At first they had been polite, removing their hats and asking courteously if they were on the right road to the town of Blanco.

"You are," she told them. "Straight ahead for a mile and a half."

They thanked her, and that was when the big one looked around. "Kinda deserted to be so near town," he said. "What do you think, Jink?"

"Trees over there," the one called Jink said. "Be a little cooler. Nobody'd see us there. Nobody'd bother us."

The big one put his hat back on. Then he pulled a pistol from the holster at his side and leveled it at

Ellie. "If you'll guide your team over there to the trees, ma'am, we can get on with our business."

Ellie didn't understand, not at first. She thought they intended to rob her. "There's nothing of value here. Just groceries. If you're hungry, you're welcome to take whatever you want."

Jink grinned, his mouth a thin slit in his face. "We'll do that, all right, ma'am. Let me help you along there."

He rode over and grabbed the reins out of her hands, guiding the mules toward the grove of trees.

When they got there, the bigger of the two men ordered Ellie into the back of the wagon and pulled his horse alongside. When he stepped into the wagon, she sensed for the first time what was about to happen.

"Don't," she said. "Please."

He reached out and pulled her backwards off the wagon seat and threw her into the bed. She screamed then and tried to twist away, as if hiding herself under the wagon seat would help.

The big man laughed and reached out for her, and she kicked at him, her foot striking him on the shin, but he just laughed louder and pointed the pistol at her again. When she looked at the menacing barrel aimed at her head, looking as big around as the mouth of a cannon, she stopped screaming.

She didn't remember much after that, but it was more than she wanted to remember.

She felt the big man's scratchy beard rubbing

against her face, and she smelled the stink of his breath, the stale, sweaty reek of his body.

She shuddered at the tearing sound of her clothing, and she blinked back tears at the sharp fierce pain when he penetrated her. She felt something tearing inside her, and she felt the blood running down the inside of her legs.

She heard the rustling of his sweat-stiff shirt, the sound of his rutting.

She closed her eyes and lay still, biting her lip to keep from crying out. She would not give him the pleasure of knowing he had hurt her.

Her face burned with shame now at the thought of it, and she shook her head, still cradled in her hands, from side to side. But her eyes remained dry.

She looked at the groceries scattered around in the wagon bed, and she began crawling around to gather them up. She worked methodically, picking up each can, holding it in front of her eyes and trying to decide whether it was fruit or tomatoes, then putting it back into the bag it had come from. There wasn't much she could do about the coffee, but she tried to gather up most of the pinto beans.

When she had everything back in the bag from the store, she reached under the seat for her bonnet, which had come off in her first struggles. She smoothed her hair as best she could, put on the bonnet, and tied it under her chin.

Then she stood up, ignoring the weakness in her

knees and the pain between her legs. She climbed back into the wagon seat and retrieved the reins.

The two mules looked back at her, twitching their ears without curiosity. They took no interest in what had happened. They might have wondered about the unscheduled stop, but the rest of the day's events had no effect on them.

She jerked their heads around and got them started back to the road. Then she headed them toward home.

The woman had been Ben's idea.

"Why the hell not?" Jink said when Ben made his suggestion.

That was the way they lived their lives, from moment to moment. They thought mostly about their immediate desires and very little about the consequences of gratifying those desires in whatever way they wanted to.

They'd killed and robbed a drifter in Arkansas once and taken two dollars off his body. It hadn't been money they were after, though. They'd killed him because they could, because there was no one around to stop them.

They'd killed a white man and his squaw up in the Oklahoma Territory, a couple of years back, too. Buried the bodies in back of the man's sod house and lived there for nearly a month before they'd exhausted his liquor and food supply.

The man hadn't done anything to Ben and Jink. They'd been on the prod, and they'd just happened on the sod house one day. The man had offered them a drink of water for their horses and a meal for themselves, and Ben had shot him right in the middle of his face.

The woman had smelled like an Indian, but they'd raped her, too, before they killed her.

Jink had hoped the woman in the wagon would be pretty. At a distance there was no way to tell what she looked like under her bonnet, but Jink decided it didn't matter. Any woman was bound to be better than none, and maybe this one wouldn't smell like a damn Indian.

Besides, it had been a long time since Jink had had a woman, any woman at all, Indian or not, and a hell of a lot longer since he'd had one that he hadn't paid for. The last one like that had been the Indian woman, come to think of it.

The idea of taking the woman right there out in the open, in her own wagon, had excited Jink, and it didn't seem like much of a risk. It wasn't as if they were going to be staying on in Blanco, after all.

Now, however, riding toward the town, Jink was uncharacteristically worried. "Reckon that bitch'll cause us any trouble?" he said. "What if O'Grady finds out?"

Ben didn't seem worried at all. In fact, he seemed downright cheerful.

"In the first place," he said, "we're the ones oughta

cause *her* trouble. My knees are still hurtin' from rub-bin' against those damn planks in the wagon bed. And those beans were pretty hard on me too. Besides, ain't nobody gonna tell O'Grady, least *I* ain't. What about you?"

"Hell, no. You know better than that, Ben."

"Then how's there gonna be any trouble? You think she's gonna get up a posse and send the marshal after us? We'll be long gone before that happens."

"Maybe," Jink said. He shook his head. "You never know with women, though. You just never can tell."

"Bull," Ben said. "You can tell, all right. Besides, she enjoyed it, at least she enjoyed my part of it. Mighta enjoyed you, too, hard as that is to believe, if you hadn't slapped her around like you did."

"She bit me," Jink said.

"Didn't say I blamed you."

Jink's finger, the one he'd cut on the can lid, was hurting him, and he sucked on it for a second. He took it out of his mouth and looked at it, but it looked all right, maybe a little swollen and red, but not too bad.

"Woman that'd bite a man, no tellin' what else she might do," he said. "I think maybe we shoulda shot her. That way, we wouldn't have to worry about her tellin' anybody about what we done."

Ben was getting tired of the conversation. He reined his horse to a stop and pulled his makings from his shirt pocket. He rolled a cigarette quickly and effi-ciently, twisted the ends, and stuck it in his mouth. He plucked a match out of his hatband, struck it with a fingernail, and lit his smoke.

After a couple of puffs he said to Jink, who had reined up beside him, "Look at it this way. We've done a lot worse things before now, and the only time we got caught at 'em was our own damn fault, not some woman's. And in an hour or so we're gonna be in a hell of a lot worse trouble than any woman can give us if O'Grady's waitin' for us in Blanco like he said he'd be."

Ben was surely right about that, and Jink shut up. Still, even though he was quiet, he couldn't stop worrying about the woman. There was just something about her, something about the way she'd looked at him just before she bit him, that bothered him.

He couldn't explain what it was, and he guessed he was just being stupid. Ben was right. Considering what they were going to Blanco for, the woman didn't make much difference.

They couldn't hang a man but once.

Chapter 2

Burt Taine poured the water out of the wooden bucket onto the wilted tomato plants, but he didn't figure it would do them much good. Too late in the season, and the tomato crop hadn't worked out very well this year anyway. First it was the birds, and then it was the bugs. He was lucky to get a single tomato for himself and Ellie. He hoped she'd bring a few cans from the store. He was a man who liked a tomato now and then.

Taine wasn't tall, but he was broad, wide across the shoulders and thick through the chest. He strained the buttons of his work shirts, and the muscles of his arms bulged the sleeves as he poured the water. He watched it soak into the parched ground and then turned to carry the bucket back to the well.

On his way, he shaded his eyes and looked up at the sun. It was getting on toward late afternoon, and he wondered why Ellie hadn't come back from town yet.

Taine wasn't really worried that his wife was a little late in coming back. There were any number of things that could have delayed her. Maybe Alf Rogers had showed her some new bolts of cloth at the mercantile store, or maybe she had run into someone to talk to, some woman she knew from the church who'd invited her to stop by for a cup of coffee or tea. Ellie liked to get away from the farm now and then and talk to someone about something other than the latest crop or whether it was going to rain in time to save the corn or what the price of cattle would be when the next calves were ready for market.

Burt didn't blame her. He liked to get away himself now and then. They'd spent six years now, six hard years, trying to hang on and make a living by running a small farm and ranching operation, and it hadn't been easy.

They raised enough food for their own needs and still often had enough left over to sell in town, though by this late in the summer most of the garden was played out, which was why Ellie had to do some shopping every week.

Now and then the livestock they raised did more than pay their own way, too, but when you came right down to it, Burt and Ellie didn't have a lot to call their own. They had a small account in the Merchants' Bank in Blanco, and they kept their debts paid at Rogers' Mercantile and Andrews' Feed and Seed, but no one could say they lived high on the hog.

Maybe it was a blessing that they'd never had children, though Burt was sure that Ellie wanted them. She often said that it didn't matter to her, but he could tell that there was a longing in her, just as there was in him. He would have liked strong sons or daughters to help him around the place and for the company they'd be, but he knew that a larger family would also mean extra trouble and expense.

Ellie, of course, was more of a help than anyone would think. She was almost as strong as a man, and she didn't mind putting her hand to a plow. She could work right beside Burt in the hottest sun or the coldest rain and do almost as much as he could.

She wasn't the prettiest woman in the country, not by a long shot, but she was the best woman there was as far as Burt was concerned. He knew as well as anyone the truth of the saying about beauty being only skin deep.

She was a woman who could take care of herself, too, and that was another reason why Burt wasn't worried. They lived only a few miles out of town, and there wasn't anything much that could happen between Blanco and the farm. He kept the wagon in good repair, and even if something had gone wrong with it, unlikely as that was, Ellie was perfectly capable of walking the distance to the farm. She was a good walker, and as far as Burt knew she never tired.

So he wasn't worried, not even though an hour or more passed beyond her usual arrival time. Burt had plenty to do to keep his mind and hands occupied. There was a leak in the roof that he'd been meaning to fix, and his saddle horse needed a new shoe on his right forefoot. There was a cracked board in the front porch that he wanted to replace before it gave way and tripped somebody up, and the pulley on the well needed greasing. It had screamed like a lovesick cat when he drew up the bucket of water for the parched tomatoes.

He was standing on the edge of the well when Ellie drove the wagon into the yard. He could tell right off that there was something wrong by the stiff way she was sitting, staring straight ahead as if there was something that she was looking at but that no one else could see.

Burt wiped the grease off his hand onto a rag that he jammed into his back pocket. He jumped down and went over to meet Ellie, but she drove the mules straight past him, nearly running him down with the wagon.

When the wagon was in front of the house, she jerked back on the rein so hard that she pulled the mules' heads up and back. They planted their feet, and the wagon came to a halt in a cloud of white dust.

Ellie climbed slowly and stiffly down from the wagon seat. Burt came running up, wondering what the trouble was, and put out a hand to help her.

Ellie looked at him with unseeing eyes and slapped at his hand, knocking it aside.

"Ellie," he said. He could see an angry red mark on her face, and there was still a little blood on her lip. "What's the matter?"

She brushed past him and stepped up on the porch, not even noticing that he'd mended the cracked board. She reached out and braced herself against one of the posts that held up the porch covering.

Burt saw the dark stain of the blood on the back of her dress.

"Ellie," he said again, reaching out his hand once more.

She looked at him with hard black eyes. "Don't touch me," she said.

Ben and Jink sat at a table in the rear of the White Dog Saloon, the only drinking establishment in the town of Blanco. They'd each had a shot of whiskey in the bar and then retired with the bottle to the table to await the expected arrival of Daniel O'Grady.

Their connection with O'Grady went back nearly ten years, to the time they'd all served together in the state's prison at Huntsville.

O'Grady was an Irishman who had left the old country for reasons unspecified and wound up in Texas. He had bright blue eyes that sparkled with humor even in the decidedly unpleasant confines of the prison walls, and hair of a faded red that he swore had burned in the sun like the flames of a summer brush fire when he was a younger man.

"Ah, and didn't the women love me for it, too,"

he said. "Many's the one of them I led down the garden path in my salad days."

In Texas, however, O'Grady, now in his late thirties and well past his salad days, had fallen on hard times. Money was hard to come by, and he had several times found himself forced to resort to illegal means to obtain it. Oddly enough, or at least it seemed odd to Ben and Jink, he seemed to regret his transgressions. His illegal money-making activities, however, whatever they might have been, were not the reason he found himself in prison.

He was there because he had shot and killed a man in a bar fight, which ordinarily wouldn't have been the kind of thing to land a man in the pen, except that unfortunately the man had been shot three times in the back after he'd whipped O'Grady around the saloon, knocked him into a heap in a corner and turned to get his pistol off the floor where it had fallen and finish the job.

O'Grady never considered claiming self-defense. He did, however, think he could avoid serving any time in prison if he could only get out of the saloon and onto his horse under his own power.

He had his pistol out, after all, and he had demonstrated a certain willingness to use it that had not gone unnoticed by the witnesses to his actions. The witnesses weren't likely the kind of men who would've tried to prevent an armed and dangerous gunman from making a precipitous exit, but unluckily for O'Grady, his now-deceased opponent had somehow in the heat of the fighting managed to dislocate O'Grady's right kneecap. When O'Grady tried to stand, he had fallen back to the floor, landing flat on his face and dropping his pistol in the process.

When the local lawmen arrived on the scene, most of the witnesses who were still sober at that time of the night had fled the scene, leaving O'Grady where he lay. O'Grady had thought of pleading self-defense then, but it had not saved him from sentencing.

Ben and Jink, despite their penchant for casual criminal acts, were residing in Huntsville for a much lesser offense than that for which O'Grady had been convicted, having been caught after a badly bungled attempt to rob a small-town bank. They had made the absurd amateur mistake of doing their robbery on the Fourth of July.

"Sweet Jesus," O'Grady said when they had told him about it. "Sure and you'd be knowing that there wouldn't be a solitary soul around to let you into the vault on a day like that, what with the celebrating and the drinking that must have been going on."

Ben and Jink hadn't thought of that, to tell the truth, but that was only the first of their mistakes. Thoughtless action, not planning, was their trademark.

They had thought only of the fact that most of the town's able-bodied population would be so busy celebrating and picnicking that two would-be bank robbers would have the whole place to themselves and that they could clean out the vault at their leisure.

"It should've worked, too," Jink said. "We had dynamite, and we blew that bank wide open."

"Ah, but they must've heard you," O'Grady said. "Dynamite, now, it's not a quiet device."

"We thought about that," Ben said. "We were gonna set it off during the fireworks."

O'Grady shook his head. "Having the banker on hand is a touch easier, I'd think. And much less of a strain on the nervous system, too, I might add."

"Yeah, well, we know that now," Ben said. "But the dynamite seemed like a good idea when we thought of it."

"And what went wrong?" O'Grady said. "If you don't mind the asking."

"It wasn't our fault," Jink said.

That was one way of looking at it. He and Ben had timed things to coincide with the fireworks, but had either of them taken the trouble to inquire, they might have learned that the town's fireworks had not arrived in time for the scheduled patriotic celebration, and therefore the announced display did not take place as advertised, throwing into disarray all Ben and Jink's careful planning.

Instead, the peaceful darkness of the early holiday evening was shattered by the noise of the exploding dynamite, which blew out all the windows of the bank, shifted the roof, and weakened the support walls, without, however, doing much damage to the vault itself.

The explosion, of course, called undue attention to the bank, and while Ben and Jink had not lingered after seeing the unsuccessful result of their attempt, they had not gotten far before being overtaken by the marshal and a hastily organized posse.

O'Grady shook his head sympathetically. "It takes a certain knowledge of explosives for getting dynamite to work properly. An uncertain device, as I said, as well as a loud one."

"Yeah," Ben said. "Next time, we'll know better."

"If there is a next time," Jink said, convinced that there never would be.

And there had not been until now. Ben and Jink had finished their sentences and left the prison to resume their errant ways, though they stuck to the kind of random murder, rape, and robbery that, if not as profitable as robbing a bank might have been was at least the sort of criminal activity for which they had so far gone unpunished. They were content to leave the more ambitious crimes to those who demonstrated more aptitude for them.

O'Grady, along with two other men, had escaped from prison not long after the release of Ben and Jink. His two companions had been caught almost immediately, but O'Grady had eluded his pursuers and set off for parts unknown.

Occasionally his path happened to cross that of Ben and Jink, and O'Grady had once expressed to them his desire to succeed where they had failed—to rob a bank and make off with a large sum of money.

"If you need any help, let us know," Ben told him.

"Just as long as there ain't no damn dynamite involved."

"There won't be any of that," O'Grady said. "You can rest assured on that point."

They had lost track of him after that, but recently they had run across him again, in Texas, of all places.

"Never thought we'd be seein' you in this state again," Jink told him over a drink one night in a border-town saloon.

O'Grady had eyed one of the prostitutes that frequented the saloon they were in and tipped his nearly empty glass in her direction.

"Ah well. Mexico was restful, but restfulness is often overrated," he said. "And where would I find such lovely women as that one but in the grand state of Texas?"

"Yeah," Ben said, though the woman must have been well past fifty and had wrinkles that her heavy powder could not completely cover. "But what about the law?"

"And what about the law?" O'Grady said. "Surely by now they harbor no memory of Daniel O'Grady and his sins, however vicious they may have been."

Ben and Jink weren't so sure of that. They didn't trust the law to forget anything.

"Besides," O'Grady went on, "the time has come for me to satisfy my ambition to become a rich man."

Jink perked up at that. He leaned his thin frame across the table. "How're you gonna do that?" he said.

And that was when O'Grady told them about the bank in the little town of Blanco.

"It's one of those small-town banks that has more than its share of money," he said. "All because of one rich man who lives there, hoarding more money than he could ever spend, even if he lived his evil old life for another hundred years."

"Rich men don't take it too good when you rob them," Ben said. "They don't like to lose what they've held on to for so long."

"Ah, but that's the good part," O'Grady said. "This particular rich man is not going to live another hundred years. He's not going to live much more than a month if the doctors can be trusted. And he is, so I've been told, in no condition to do a thing about the loss of his money except to regret it."

"Huh," Jink said. He didn't trust doctors any more than he trusted the law.

"Yeah," Ben said, as if Jink had made some profound comment on the human condition. "And what about his family? They ain't gonna like us takin' his money out of that bank any more than he would, I reckon."

"Sure and that's another good part of the story," O'Grady said. "His only family is a worthless son who desperately wants the old man's money."

"That's what I meant," Ben said.

"To continue," O'Grady said as if Ben had not interrupted, "the son wants the money, but he has no way of getting it at the old man's death, since the old man has disinherited him in favor of some charity home for orphans in New York City."

"I don't get it," Ben said.

"I do," Jink said, his thin lips smiling. "You met the son, I guess, O'Grady."

"Oh, yes, that I did. In Mexico, it was. He was there to partake of the pleasures of the flesh while he still had some limited access to his father's money, and it was there he told me the whole sad tale."

"But you figured out a way to help him," Jink said.

"True. I did that little thing."

"I still don't get it," Ben said.

"We rob the bank," Jink said. "Before the old man dies and the money gets shipped off to the orphans. And we split the money with the son." He looked at O'Grady. "Am I right?"

O'Grady smiled, his eyes twinkling. "Of course you are, old son." He put his glass to his mouth and swallowed the last of his drink. "Do you get it now, Ben?"

"Not all of it," Ben said.

O'Grady looked concerned. "Which part of it is it that you're still not grasping?"

"That part about splittin' the money," Ben said. "I'm not graspin' that part at all."

Chapter 3

—•—✠—•—

Gerald Crossland sat in the front room of the ranch house where he lived with his father and smoked his cigar. His father hated the cigars and claimed that the smoke interfered with his breathing. It might even have been true, but Gerald didn't care if it was. The old man was good for at least two more weeks, cigars or no cigars, if the doctor was to be believed.

Two weeks was more than enough from Gerald's point of view, a damn sight more than the old man deserved. In fact, after today the old man could die anytime he damn well pleased. After today, Gerald wouldn't care anymore.

He got up from his chair and walked across the room, moving with a strange gracefulness for a short man whose frame was sheathed in soft, quivering fat. He was obviously not accustomed to hard work, and his pale skin indicated his preference for remaining indoors.

When he reached the open door of his father's bedroom, he paused and blew smoke through the doorway. There was no sound from the room, so Gerald stepped inside.

There were heavy drapes over the window and the light in the room was dim. Gerald's father, Jonathan, his eyes closed, lay quietly on the single bed, covered by a thin sheet that rose and fell slowly with his breathing.

Gerald stood and looked at him. The old man had really been something in his own day, Gerald had to admit that much. Jonathan Crossland had been the kind of man who was able to coax a fortune out of the cattle market through years of hard work and sheer force of will.

But that day was past, and what had the hard work and determination gotten him? A wasting disease that sapped his strength, robbed him of his once considerable energy and was now about to kill him.

Well, Gerald reflected, that wasn't quite fair. The hard work had also gotten Jonathan the fortune that Gerald so coveted, most of which was currently on deposit in the Blanco bank, old Jonathan preferring to have his money near to home. And the force of his determination was the only thing keeping Jonathan alive now, though it wouldn't for much longer.

Gerald had inherited none of his father's characteristics, except possibly the determination. He did not know where his size and laziness had come from. He could not remember his mother, who had died when he was less than two years old, but he supposed those traits might have come from her. Jonathan sometimes spoke of her with remembered affection, but never with admiration.

Jonathan did not admire his son, either, and two years earlier he had taken care to see that his lack of admiration was made clear.

He had called Gerald into his room one day had handed his son a piece of paper.

"I want you to read this," he said. "It's a copy of my will."

Gerald had read it, all right. Before he was through, his hand had begun to shake and his face had turned bright red. Gerald was not only to get no money, he was to receive the ranch only with the stipulation that it not be sold.

"I can see that you understand it," Jonathan said, noting the trembling of Gerald's hand.

Gerald returned the paper to his father without speaking. He was afraid of what he might say.

"Well?" Jonathan said.

Finally Gerald managed a nod. "I understand it," he said. His voice sounded like a frog croaking.

"Fine. You know, then, that I'm not cuttin' you off with nothing. You'll get enough so that you won't starve. But if you want to live the way you've gotten used to, you're goin' to have to earn it yourself. Maybe even go to work."

Remembering his humiliation and outrage at that moment, Gerald looked at the dim form of the dying man on the bed. He took another puff of his cigar and blew a cloud of white smoke into the room.

"That's what *you* think, old man," he said.

When Daniel O'Grady walked into the White Dog Saloon, his dusty hat was pulled low over his face. He did not stop at the bar but walked straight to the back of the room to the table where Ben and Jink were sitting.

O'Grady had made one big mistake in judgment in his life, and that one had cost him dearly. He had thought a judge and jury would understand that the man he had shot in the back was not just walking away. He was going for his pistol and putting some distance between himself and O'Grady so that when he turned and fired, it would look as if he had done so in response to some word or action of O'Grady's. O'Grady had been more conscious than the man had realized and had taken advantage of that fact to be the first one to shoot.

The judge hadn't seen things the way O'Grady had, however, and not even the dead man's vile reputation did anything to change the judge's mind.

So O'Grady's mistake in judgment had put him behind the prison walls. He had sworn to himself then that he would never make another one. He hoped that he was not doing that now by joining forces with Ben and Jink.

He believed that he could trust the two men; he

just hoped that they could carry through their part of the action. They were certainly brave enough, if brave was the word; unimaginative was probably more like it. What worried O'Grady was the matter of their capability. In his estimate, they were likely to be unpredictable in a pinch.

He would have tried the bank alone but for the fact that he was not a man given to taking unnecessary chances with his own life and well-being. He did not believe that robbing the bank in Blanco posed any great threat to him, but on the other hand it was always best to have someone standing behind you just in case someone else decided to try redeeming a misspent life by attempting to perform a heroic action, no matter how ill-advised it might be under the circumstances.

So O'Grady wanted someone to guard his back, and Ben and Jink were as likely as anyone he could think of. Truth to tell, a man like O'Grady, having spent so many years on the run, was not apt to know a great many dependable people.

That was a situation that O'Grady sometimes regretted. He liked to think that he was an honest man at heart, having resorted to crime only when all legitimate means of obtaining a living had been exhausted. He had never intended to spend his life in the company of men like Ben Atticks and Jink Howard. He was hoping that the bank robbery would allow him to occupy the rest of his days in better surroundings than those of the White Dog Saloon, and with a better class of men.

"God save all here," he said as he sat at the table.

"Howdy, Daniel," Ben said. "You think God would mind us havin' a drink or two?" He indicated the bottle.

"Not the God of the Irish," O'Grady said, looking to see if there was a glass for him. There was, and he filled it gratefully.

"Cuts the dust," he said after a deep swallow.

He looked at the two men and noticed that Jink had a piece of dirty cloth tied around one finger. The cloth was stained a rusty red with blood.

"And what might that be?" he said, gesturing at the finger before draining his glass.

"Just a little cut," Jink said. He had tied it up when it had started bleeding again in the saloon. "It's nothin'."

"Sure and I hope you're right about that," O'Grady said.

Ben wasn't one for small talk about the general health of his partners. "Is it on?" he said.

"As certain as the night that follows day," O'Grady said. He reached into a pocket of his stained vest, pulled out a worn nickel-plated watch and opened the cover. "One hour from now, to be exact." He snapped the cover shut and replaced the watch in the vest.

"One hour?" Ben said. "That doesn't give us much time to get ready."

"Time is something that we don't need," O'Grady said. "There's no reason for us to linger about here in town and let people get too good a look at our faces, and for what we're going to do, there's no getting ready."

"That fella you told us about," Ben said. "Is he gonna pull his weight?"

"Why of course he is," O'Grady said. "It's all a part of the plan."

But he wished that he was as confident of Gerald Crossland as he sounded.

Jonathan Crossland had been merely feigning sleep to avoid having to talk to his son, not that Gerald would have spoken to him in any case. Jonathan hadn't slept for quite a while, not well, and not for more than four or five minutes at a time, anyhow. The pain was too bad, though he would never give Gerald the satisfaction of knowing that.

The laudanum that the doctor had given Jonathan was practically useless at this point. It had helped a great deal at first, easing the pain and making Jonathan almost forget that he was a sick man, but as the days went on it had done less and less for him, other than give him quite colorful dreams during those short spans that it affected him at all. At this point in his illness, it had hardly any more effect on him than drinking water.

When Gerald left the room, the old man's eyes opened, and his nose twitched with pleasure at the smell of the cigar smoke. He had told Gerald that he didn't like it, but that was a lie. He had taken great satisfaction in smoking when he had been able, and now that he was not, the only way he could enjoy it was to smell the smoke exhaled by others. Gerald would never have dreamed of smoking in the room had he known that Jonathan enjoyed it, however, so Jonathan had told him the opposite.

As he lay there on the hard bed, Jonathan could feel the fever that raged in him like an unabated fire, but he refused to let it cloud his mind. He fought it every minute, with all the strength he had left.

It was not an easy battle. His body felt light under the covers, so light that he wondered why he did not float up from the bed so high that he could reach out a hand and touch the rough wooden rafters of the room.

It was as if the thin blanket that covered him was the only thing holding him there, though he supposed it was actually the pain that dragged him down, the pain that was so much a part of him that he had to grit his teeth against it to keep it from erupting from his mouth in a great bellow of anguish.

It was just as well that he had to keep his mouth shut, he told himself. Otherwise, he might have told Gerald something that the worthless little son of a bitch didn't have any business knowing.

Jonathan's mouth twisted in a grimace that might have been an attempt at a smile as he thought about the words Gerald had spoken just before leaving.

You're wrong, Gerald, he thought. *It's not what I think that matters. It's what I* know.

———

Saddling the horse in the barn was as hard a physical labor as Gerald ever intended to perform again as long as he lived, and for him it *was* labor.

He was not used to being out of the ranch house, where the thick adobe walls kept out a great deal of the day's heat, and he was not used to getting the animal to stand still and accept the bridle, heaving the heavy saddle up onto the horse's back and tightening the girth.

It might have been easier if the horse had been inclined to cooperate, but it was not. It had not been saddled often during the weeks of Jonathan's illness, and it had not been saddled by Gerald in much longer than that.

There had been a time when the ranch had employed men to perform such menial tasks, but now there was no one left except for one old Mexican woman who cooked and took care of Jonathan. The old man had decided that if he was going to die, there was no need to pay people to hang around the place and do meaningless jobs or, worse than that, do nothing at all.

The hardest part of the job Gerald had to do was to mount the horse. His bulk made the job harder than it should have been, but he finally located a small empty nail keg and stood it beside the horse. Stepping up onto the keg, he managed to get a foot in the stirrup and then swing his other leg across the horse's back.

Once mounted, Gerald was a good rider, though

he looked somewhat ridiculous because of his bulk. The horse did not seem to mind the rider's size, however. Having been saddled, it resigned itself to the rider and moved docilely off in the direction of town.

Gerald told himself that everything would go well. He was not worried so much about what he was to do, or about what the others were to do.

His own job was easy, and if the man he had met in Mexico showed up, things should go well enough. The man had seemed a competent sort. And if he did not show up, then Gerald had really lost nothing, having had nothing in the first place since everything was going to that damned orphanage.

If the man got caught, that would be another problem, but only if he revealed Gerald's name, in which case Gerald planned to deny everything. There was really nothing that could be proved against him, after all, and once again he would lose nothing.

So he was not worried about the big things; he was worried instead about the things that should have been the simplest, such as getting away. That in itself was not going to be the problem, he knew, but since he had not been able to bring along the nail keg, mounting the horse again was going to be the difficult part. If he could do that, he would have no trouble escaping before any pursuit could be organized, if indeed anyone thought of pursuit at all. More than likely, they would not.

Gerald smiled.

They wouldn't think of coming after him because

they would have plenty of other things to occupy their minds.

"So that's all there is to it?" Ben said, pouring another drink from the bottle that was now almost empty.

"That's all there is," O'Grady said. "For you two at least. You just hold your guns, make sure that no one walks in on us or gets away. I'll be the one to do the talking. It's more in the way of my sort of thing."

"I just thought of somethin'," Jink said. "That guy whose old man has all that money. What if he gets caught and tells them your name?"

"Ah, but for that to happen he would have to be knowing my name, now wouldn't he?" O'Grady said.

"You didn't tell him?" Jink said, as if such an expedient would never have occurred to him.

"Of course I told him," O'Grady said. "I told him that I was a wandering Scotsman by the name of Jack MacLane, kicked out of the clan for behavior unbecoming one who wore the tartan, and down on my luck in Mexico. There was more to the story, I believe, but I'm afraid I don't recall it now."

Ben shook his head with admiration, only some of which was inspired by the drink he was holding. "I gotta hand it to you, Daniel. You're a natural-born liar."

O'Grady smiled. "Sure and I thank you for the compliment," he said.

Chapter 4

———◆◆◆◆———

Burt Taine's tanned face was mottled with white and his fists were clenched at his sides.

"What did they look like, Ellie?" he said. "Tell me, goddammit."

Ellie sat in a straight-backed wooden chair at the table where they ate their meals. Her hands were resting on the table in front of her, and she was looking at the backs of them as if there might be a message written there that only she could see and understand. She might not have heard her husband for all the indication she gave.

Ben stepped over to the side of the table opposite her and slammed his fist down on it.

Ellie herself did not move, but her hands bounced with the force of the blow. She raised her head, but her eyes did not meet Burt's. She stared at a spot somewhere just over his left shoulder.

"What did they look like?" he said again.

When she spoke, her voice was flat and toneless. "One of them was big and had a beard," she said. "One of them was skinny and had beady eyes."

"What else?" Burt said.

She lowered her head and stared at the backs of her hands again. "I can't remember," she said.

Burt wanted to scream out his rage. He wanted to kick a hole in the wall or pound his fist through the table. It was as if a fire were burning in his belly, and he felt as though his head had swollen to twice its normal size. It was a wonder that his eyes didn't pop out and roll on the floor.

He shuddered and took a deep breath. Then he said, "I'm going after them."

Ellie didn't respond. She didn't even look up. She looked at the backs of her hands, turned them over and looked at the palms. They were hard and callused, the hands of a woman who knew what hard work was.

"I said I'm going after them," Burt told her. He went over to where his gunbelt hung from a peg on the wall and took it down. He did not look at his wife while he strapped it on.

He didn't remember the last time he had used the pistol, which was an old Navy Colt. He was a farmer and a rancher, and in the normal course of things he had little use for guns. He had never used the pistol either for defense or intimidation, though he had once killed a rattler with it, and once he had used it to kill a coyote that was stealing their chickens.

In the case of the coyote, he had gotten lucky and

hit it with his third shot. The snake, being a considerably smaller target, had required that he empty the whole cylinder.

He tried to put such thoughts out of his mind. When a man's wife had been raped, there was nothing a man could do but strap on his gun and go after the men who had violated her.

If he could find them, he would face them. If he couldn't find them, he could at least tell Marshal Dawson what had happened and put the marshal on their trail.

Burt buckled the gunbelt and jammed his battered hat on his head. "I'll be back by dark," he said.

Ellie still stared at her hands. A fly landed on one and crawled across the upturned palm. She made no move to shake it off.

"Did you hear me?" Burt said.

"I heard you," she said.

She felt strangely detached from the proceedings. Once, when she was a girl before she had ever met Burt Taine, her parents had taken her to see a real play in a real theater, and she felt now as she had felt then, as if she were sitting in a strange room watching the actions of strangers on a stage, actions which were interesting to her in a vague way but which had no real bearing on her own life.

Burt took the double-barreled shotgun from its place by the wall and checked to see that it was loaded. It was, and he laid it on the table in front of Ellie.

"Don't let anyone in the house," he said, worried that her attackers might for some reason find their way there. "If anyone tries to get in, you let him have both barrels."

Ellie reached out a hand, and the fly rose in the air and buzzed away. Ellie ran her hand over the cool dark barrels of the shotgun.

"You understand me?" Burt said.

"I understand."

He wasn't sure that she did, but he went out the door without looking back, passing through the shade of the porch and out into the hard sunlight of the yard.

Ellie thought that he looked like an actor in the play making his exit and that like the actor he was merely performing a role, doing what was expected of him because people would have thought it strange had he done anything else.

It was as if what had happened to her was not his real motivation; he was moved instead by some sense of obligation to behave the way everyone would think he should.

Ellie heard the hoofbeats as he rode away toward town, but she did not rise from the table to watch him leave.

By the time Gerald Crossland arrived at Whistler's Livery, he was sweating freely. Streams of sweat ran from under his hat and down his fat red cheeks. His shirt was soaked—front, back, and under the arms.

Where his body met the leather saddle, there was a slick coating of sweat. He was looking forward to getting out of the saddle, no matter how much trouble he might have getting back in.

Though the sun was still bright in the sky, Gerald could see black clouds massing heavily in the north, and there was the slight stirring of a fresh breeze. Ordinarily, Gerald would have welcomed the relief, but because of what he was about to do, he did not look forward to the possibility of rain.

Whistler's was on the south edge of town, a little apart from the small business district, and Gerald had come to it by a roundabout way, arriving behind the stable and out of sight of anyone passing by the front. He was also out of sight of Earl Whistler, the owner, who generally sat tipped back in a wooden chair in the shade just inside the big double door in front when he wasn't busy with the animals in his care.

It was important that Gerald not be seen, since he intended to burn the stable to the ground, or at least create an inferno of a size sufficient to draw most of the population of Blanco to the scene.

This part of the plan had been Gerald's idea. He would create a diversion that would allow the robbery of the bank to proceed smoothly and without any aggravating interruptions by the marshal. The bank was in the center of town, at least a quarter of a mile from the livery stable, and with luck and with everyone's attention concentrated on the fire, the robbery would go practically unnoticed until it was all over.

Gerald dismounted behind the stable. He wiped his face with his bandanna and stood quietly for a few seconds to get his breath. Even minor exertions were hard for him, but he soon recovered.

He was standing beside the pile of dirty hay and straw that Whistler, who was notoriously tidy for a livery stable owner, added to every morning when he cleaned the place. Every week or so, Whistler would load the pile on a wagon and haul it somewhere out of town and dump it in a gully, but he had not done so recently.

It had not rained in Blanco for quite some time, and the sun had sucked all the moisture from all the hay, except for a small portion of the topmost layer.

Gerald looked to the north sky at the thick black clouds gathering there. Lightning flickered through them, changing their color momentarily from black to purple, and there was a dim crack of thunder. The clouds were still quite a way off, however, and Gerald thought there would be plenty of time for the fire to have its intended effect before it started raining hard enough to have any result.

He got a damp cigar from his shirt, lit it, and threw the match into the straw. Then he threw in two more matches for good measure.

The straw smoldered for a moment and then burst into bright orange flames.

Gerald watched until the fire had spread to the back wall of the stable. Then he tried to mount the horse, but the difficult job was made even harder by the fact that the horse was spooked by the fire. It danced to the left and to the right, slamming into Gerald, who was clinging to the reins, and nearly knocking him to the dirt.

Gerald resisted the urge to draw his pistol and kill the horse. That would be stupid. He took the cigar that he had clamped between his teeth and threw it on the ground.

"Easy, boy," Gerald said to the horse in what he hoped was a soothing tone. "Easy."

The horse didn't pay any attention to his words or his tone. It kept dancing from side to side and pulling backward on the reins.

The back wall of the stable was burning now, crackling, popping. There was still no alarm from the front, and Gerald had an idea.

"Come along, boy," he said, leading the horse away from the fire. "Come along. We'll get out of here."

After a brief struggle, he was able to lead the horse away from the fire and around to the front of the stable. Sure enough, old Whistler had gone to sleep in his chair. His eyes were closed, his head was back, and he had no idea that the whole stable was about to burn down around him. His snoring was almost loud enough to drown out the noise of the fire.

Gerald was going to wake Whistler and warn him about the fire. No one would ever guess that Gerald was the one who had started the fire. He would save

Whistler and be a hero; no one would suspect his part in the robbery.

"Wake up, Whistler!" Gerald yelled, shaking the man by the shoulder.

Whistler jerked away, looking around to the right and left. "What the hell?" he said. "What's goin' on here?"

"Your place is on fire," Gerald said. "We've got to get the horses out!"

Whistler jumped up with surprising vigor. "Goddamn!" he said.

He turned to see the stable filling with smoke. Both men could hear the cries of frightened horses.

"Goddamn!" Whistler repeated. "You sound the alarm! I'll get them horses out!"

That suited Gerald just fine.

When Gerald spread word of the fire, even most of the customers in the White Dog Saloon responded quickly, leaping up and running for the front door. Even the bartender hustled out, taking off his stained white apron and tossing it on the bar.

O'Grady and his partners stayed in their chairs and watched them go.

"Guess that means it's time," Ben said when the last one had left.

"Right you are," O'Grady said. "So let's be going about our business."

The three of them rose and walked casually outside. The street was filled with running men, women, and children, all heading in the direction of the stable, from which orange flames rose and black smoke poured.

The sky was overcast now, making the flames seem even brighter, and thunder rumbled in the north.

"Gonna rain," Jink said. "Goddammit."

"Not before our little job is done," O'Grady said, eyeing the clouds. "Not if we do it now."

Everyone was concentrating on the fire, and no one paid any attention to the three men who sauntered across the street and into the bank. Three well-dressed men who had no inclination to dirty their suits by fighting fires were standing outside the bank, looking in the direction of the stable. They were talking among themselves and did not seem to notice the three men who entered the bank, pulling bandannas up over the lower halves of their faces as they did so.

Ben closed the door quietly behind them when they were inside. He and Jink already had their guns drawn.

"God save all here," O'Grady said. His voice boomed off the walls, hardly muffled at all by the bandanna, but there were only two people to hear him, one woman who was standing at the teller's window and the teller himself.

The woman opened her mouth to scream, but O'Grady said, "Ah, now, that wouldn't be a good idea, would it. Might cause someone to get hurt. Best be calm, and we'll be going soon."

The woman looked at him as if surprised to hear a robber talking so rationally and coolly under the circumstances. She shut her mouth slowly.

"And you, my friend," O'Grady said to the teller, "you'll be letting us into the vault, if you please."

The teller was a scrawny young man with slicked-down hair and wire-rimmed glasses. He was not intimidated by O'Grady. "I can't do that," he said. "Only Mr. Wiley can do that, and he's not here."

"Sure and that's a shame," O'Grady said. "And where might Mr. Wiley be, then?"

The teller clamped his thin lips together and said nothing.

O'Grady glanced at Ben. "Go outside and invite the three gentlemen we saw there to come inside," he said. "We wouldn't want them to be getting wet if it rains."

Ben opened the door and went out. The three men were still talking about the fire, and there was quite a crowd gathered at the livery stable now. Ben figured that just about the whole town must be there, throwing buckets of water at the flames and doing not a damn bit of good.

The wind had picked up considerably, and the thunder was rolling loudly. The rain was going to do more to put out the fire than the townspeople, but there wasn't going to be much left of the stable when the rain finally fell.

Ben tapped one of the men on the shoulder. "Why

don't you fellas come inside?" he said. "You ain't helpin' any with that fire."

They turned and stepped back in surprise at seeing his face covered. He let them have a look at his pistol.

"Just don't make no noise," he said. "Not that it'd do you any good if you did."

"Here, now," the man in the middle said. He was stout and red-faced, taller than the other two. "You can't do this."

"I'm doin' it," Ben said. "Get inside." He jerked his pistol barrel in the direction of the bank door.

The three men looked at one another helplessly and filed inside. Ben closed the door.

"Welcome to you all," O'Grady said. "And which of you might be Mr. Wiley?"

None of the men said anything.

"I bet it's this 'un," Ben said, prodding the stout man in the middle of the back with his pistol and causing him to step forward. "He's the one likes to talk."

"I'm pleased to make your acquaintance, Mr. Wiley," O'Grady said. "I know you'll be wanting us to go on our way, which we will as soon as you open your vault for us."

"No," Wiley said. "I can't do that."

"Ah, but you can," O'Grady said. "And you will. I know you wouldn't want anything to be happening to one of your customers, now would you?"

He walked over to the woman by the teller's window and put his pistol under her chin. When she started to open her mouth, he cocked the hammer.

"Now, now," he told her. "No talking." He looked back at the banker. "Well, Mr. Wiley?"

"All right," Wiley said.

"That's what I wanted to hear," O'Grady told him.

Chapter 5

———— ✦ ————

Gerald Crossland wiped his eyes with the back of his grimy hand and tried to cough the smoke out of his lungs.

He didn't know how he'd gotten roped into helping fight the fire, but he couldn't very well have refused. It would have looked bad and might have cast suspicion on him. Though he had done as little as possible, he was hotter than he'd ever been in his life, and dirtier. He found himself actually wishing that the rain would begin to fall and end his misery.

There had been only three horses boarded in the stable, along with two that Whistler rented out now and then, and Whistler had gotten them all out before Gerald had been pressed into service, not that Gerald gave a damn about any horses. He just wanted to get away from there. He'd never heard so much yelling or seen so much frenzied activity in his entire life.

Things were calming down, however, because everyone had realized that there was nothing they could do to save the stable. It was clear that no matter how much effort they put into rescuing it, the stable was going to burn to cinders and ashes, so rather than risk getting hurt or overcome by the smoke, everyone was just standing around at a safe distance and watching it burn.

It seemed to Gerald that the whole town must be there, and he was sure that the robbery had been completed successfully by now. He tried to will himself to relax and enjoy the spectacle of the burning building.

Whistler walked over to him and put a friendly hand on his shoulder.

"Good thing for them horses that you happened by, son," he said.

Whistler was even older than Gerald's father, practically toothless, and totally bald. He wore a battered hat that Gerald wouldn't even have put on a mule.

"Needed a few things from the store," Gerald said to explain his presence. "I'm glad I could be of help."

"Musta come the long way round," Whistler said.

Gerald looked at the old man sharply, but there was nothing in his face or in his voice that seemed threatening.

"Just enjoying the ride," Gerald said. "I don't get out much these days, what with my father suffering so."

"How is Mr. Crossland?" Whistler said. "He gettin' any better?"

Gerald shook his head sadly. "I'm afraid not."

"Mighty sorry to hear it," Whistler said, before walking off to talk to someone who wanted to commiserate with him about the loss of his stable.

Nosy old bastard, Gerald thought, but then the roof of the stable fell in with a whoosh and a crash, scattering sparks into the air and causing the crowd to back up in a rush of gasps and yells.

The collapse of the roof was followed by a brilliant flash of lightning and a boom of thunder from overhead, and all eyes turned to the sky.

The clouds opened up, and the rain began to fall.

Burt Taine rode hard, paying no attention to the gathering clouds, the lightning, or the thunder. He was thinking only about finding the men who had raped Ellie, and about what he was going to do if he found them.

It was always possible that they wouldn't be in Blanco at all, that they'd merely been passing by that way and not intending to stop, but somehow Burt was sure that wasn't the case.

He knew they would be there, and he knew that he would find them.

He couldn't have said how he knew, but he felt it with a certainty that went beyond explanation. It was as if all his life had been leading him to this point and that he had been living all along for the confrontation that he was sure was about to occur.

He could feel the Colt at his side, bouncing against him as he rode. He reached down his right hand and caressed the leather of the holster.

The fire that had burned inside him was gone now, replaced by something that felt like a lump of ice, hard and cold. Whatever was going to happen, he was ready for it.

The rain began just he rode into town. It came in hard, stinging drops as big as two-bit pieces. They hit the dusty street and soaked into the ground. They were widely spaced at first, but then they fell faster and harder, and the street was turning to mud before Burt had even reached the center of town. He pulled his hat lower, and water ran off the brim and onto the saddle.

Through the rain he could see a crowd gathered at the other end of the street, down where the livery stable should have been. He couldn't see the stable, however, and he wondered whether it was obscured by the curtain of rain or if something had happened to it.

Then he heard the shots from the bank.

At first, things had gone exactly as O'Grady planned. Wiley opened the vault without any further argument, and O'Grady ushered him inside.

"Hold this for me, if you please," O'Grady said, pulling a burlap bag from under his shirt and handing it to the banker. "I'll not be taking too much more of your time now."

Wiley took the bag and spread it open at the top while O'Grady began tossing in the stacked bills. When he was finished, he looked around the vault and said, "Sure and there must be more than this."

"You have it all," Wiley said. "Except whatever small amount there might be in the teller's drawer."

O'Grady had not bothered to count, but he was afraid that the money he had put into the bag could not possibly add up to the sum mentioned by Gerald Crossland, not unless there were some awfully big bills. Maybe that was the case.

"Very well," he said. "We'll call it a day, then." He took the bag from Wiley and twisted the top closed. He tied it shut with a piece of rope from his pocket. "You just stay here and rest. We'll be sending in your friends."

"You can't lock us in here," Wiley said, looking afraid for the first time. "No one but me knows the combination to the vault; we'll never get out."

"Come now," O'Grady said. "No banker would be so careless as to leave no escape for himself in such a situation. I'm sure there is someone in town who can set you at liberty sooner or later."

"No," Wiley said, though in truth he had written the combination down on a piece of paper and hidden it in his desk at home. His wife had been told of the location of the paper and would know what to do.

"Well, isn't that too bad, then?" O'Grady said,

backing out of the vault. "You can be sending the others in now," he called to Ben and Jink.

The woman and the two men who had come in with Wiley went in calmly enough. It was the teller who caused the trouble.

When the young man refused to move, Jink moved over and prodded him in the back with the pistol. When the barrel touched him, the teller turned quickly, trying to grab the pistol and snatch it from Jink's hand.

The pistol went off, and the bullet plowed into the wooden floor. The teller and Jink sprang apart. Neither of them was hurt, but the teller made the mistake of jumping for Jink a second time.

Jink jerked up the pistol and shot him in the chest.

The clerk stumbled backward and fell into the vault at the feet of the woman, who began to scream shrilly. No threat could have stopped her.

"Jesus!" O'Grady said. "I told you not to shoot!"

"You never did," Ben said. "Now hurry up and shut that vault."

O'Grady shut the door and spun the handle, cutting off the sound of the woman's screams.

"Let's get outta here," Jink said.

Burt Taine saw the three of them come out of the bank, looking both up and down the street, bandannas pulled up to cover their faces, pistols in their hands.

He knew the first two at once, even in the pouring rain.

One big, with a bit of beard sticking out over the top of the bandanna; one skinny, with beady eyes between the brim of his hat and the handkerchief that covered the lower part of his face.

The third man was behind them, and Burt had no idea who he might be. But he was as sure about the other two as if he had seen them in the wagon with Ellie, tearing her clothes away, kneeling over her.

With pressure from his left knee, he turned his horse to face them; with his right hand, he reached for his pistol.

He got it out, but he didn't get a chance to fire it.

Ben shot him first, the bullet hitting him high on the left side of his chest, throwing him back in the saddle. He held on to the reins and didn't fall from the horse.

Because his head was back and because his horse reared up, Jink's shot took him right under the chin.

The bullet went up through the roof of his mouth and, deflected slightly, through his brain and out the upper back of his skull, blowing off his hat and part of his head.

Burt fell back off the rearing horse. His fingers jerked in a reflex action, and he fired the pistol, but the bullet went harmlessly into the mud of the street. The fingers of his left hand released the reins, and he landed hard in the street, making a splatting noise in the mud. He lay there on his back, unmoving, dead before he fell.

"Jesus," O'Grady said. "Sweet Jesus."

Ben and Jink were already across the street and mounting their horses.

O'Grady followed, lugging the money bag. He looped the rope with which he'd tied it over his saddle horn and mounted up. By then, Ben and Jink were headed out of town.

There was nothing for O'Grady to do but go with them.

Marshal Rawls Dawson heard the shots and turned in time to see the man falling from his horse into the street. He also saw the three men mount their horses and ride away, but by that time he was running up the street, kicking up mud and water, headed for the bank.

The rest of the crowd, those who had not sought shelter from the rain, followed him, leaving the rain to sizzle into the ashes of the livery stable and complete the job of extinguishing the fire. There looked to be more exciting things going on.

Gerald Crossland watched the crowd surge up the street and went along behind, though he didn't exert the energy to keep up with them. He had not run in many years and he was not going to start now.

He wished that he could think of some reason to leave town, but he couldn't. And he knew that if he did leave, people would wonder why. He didn't want anyone to do that.

His clothes were soaked and stuck to him all over—wet, heavy, filthy, and uncomfortable. He had been hot before, but he was getting cold now and the rain showed no signs of letting up anytime soon.

As he walked, Gerald cursed silently.

Robbing the bank had been a risk, admittedly, but a small one. It was a risk Gerald had been willing to take. Even if the men were caught and gave his name, there was no real evidence against him, nothing more than the word of criminals. Even if things went so far as a trial, Gerald was sure nothing bad would happen to him.

But not now. Now there was a dead man. Things would never get back to normal. Gerald should never have trusted that damn MacLane, who swore there would be no killing.

Things could be worse, however. At least MacLane and his men had gotten away. Most likely they would never be caught. Gerald consoled himself with thoughts of the money that would soon be his.

Marshal Dawson looked down at the dead man. There was a circle of others gathered around and the rain streamed off their hats and shoulders.

"Goddamn, his face is a mess," someone said.

"Looks like Burt Taine, though," another man said. "What the hell was he doin' in town?"

"That don't make a damn," someone else said. "What the hell *happened* to him?"

Dawson had already figured that out. "He got in the way," he said. "Some of you men get him off the street. Take him down to Fowler's." Fowler was the undertaker.

As the men bent to pick up the body, Dawson headed for the bank, afraid of what he might find inside.

O'Grady knew that there would be a posse after them soon, and that was one good thing about the rain. No one was going to be able to track them. The rain would take care of any trail they might leave.

Nevertheless, he felt that it was a good idea to stay off the road, so they were riding through a wooded area. The rain hissed and spattered through the leaves, and the wind whipped the branches.

Ben and Jink rode up beside him.

"Where we goin'?" Ben said.

"Crossland's ranch," O'Grady said.

"I thought we talked about that," Ben said. "You said that we weren't gonna be doin' any sharin' and that we wouldn't be goin' to that ranch. You said that Crossland could just sit there and wait for us to show up, but we never would."

That had been O'Grady's original plan. Just take off with the money, head for the border, and let Crossland wish for his share.

But the killings had changed things. O'Grady needed time to think, time to come up with a new plan. Bank robbery was one thing; murder was something else.

And there was one other thing, something that O'Grady wasn't ready to discuss with his partners just yet.

"We still don't have to share," O'Grady said. "But we have to go somewhere they won't find us. They'll never look for us at that ranch."

"You better be right about that," Ben said.

O'Grady turned to face him through the rain. "Listen, you bastard, don't tell me who better be right about something. Killing those two men was stupid and unforgivable. If anything happens to us, it will be because of you and your ignorant partner."

Ben was genuinely surprised. He hadn't even thought about the killings.

"What're you gettin' so riled for?" he said. "Hell, we had to kill those fellas. There wasn't nothin' else we could do."

Oh, Lord, O'Grady thought. *What have I gotten myself into?*

Well, whatever it was, it was too late to back out of it now. He would have to make the best of it.

"How much you think we got back there?" Ben said, reaching over to pat the sack tied to O'Grady's saddle, covered now by O'Grady's slicker.

"I didn't have the time to count it," O'Grady said.

"But it's a lot, ain't it? You said it'd be a lot."

"I'm not sure," O'Grady said. "We can count it after we get to the ranch."

"You reckon they got anything to eat at that ranch?"

"We'll see," O'Grady said.

Chapter 6

The Reverend Abner Stone and his wife, Alma, were the ones who went to fetch Ellie Taine. Stone had been the Methodist minister in Blanco for seven years, and he and Alma had performed similar sad duties in the past, but that did not make what they had to do any easier.

"I only hope the poor woman has taken your sermons to heart," Alma said. Her usually cheerful round face did not have a smile on it now. "Particularly the one last week in which you touched on the comforts of the Holy Spirit."

"Or the one the week before that," Abner said, "when I preached on the wise and the foolish virgins."

"Yes," Alma said. "'For you do not know the day or the hour.'" She looked up at the clear evening sky as if there were some wisdom to be found there.

The rain had ended as suddenly as it had begun, leaving the earth churned into a sticky gumbo and the air dry and clear. The moon was rising full and yellow, and the stars were beginning to show themselves against the purple sky. The horses pulled the wagon slowly along the muddy road.

"No one is ever really prepared," Abner said. "No matter how many times you warn them."

"No," Alma said, thinking about how she would feel if someone came to her door and told her that Abner had been killed. "I suppose you're right. But Ellie is a strong woman."

"She'll have to be," Abner said.

Gerald Crossland had hardly struggled out of the saddle when O'Grady stepped out of the shadows at the back of the barn.

"Welcome home," he said.

Gerald was not surprised to see him. Gerald had given him directions to the ranch, and they had agreed to meet there and split the money. Gerald had suggested the barn as the best place for the meeting. He didn't want MacLane or anyone else involved with the robbery to come inside his house.

"Did you get it?" Gerald said.

He supposed that he should take the saddle off his horse, rub him down, and feed him, but he didn't really want to. When he got his share of the money, he would hire some hands to take care of things like that again.

O'Grady was more considerate of animals, having

had to depend on them much more often than Gerald Crossland ever had.

"Go ahead and take care of your horse," he said. "Then we'll be having us a little talk."

Gerald gave in. It took him a few minutes, but he finally got the horse stabled. Then he lit a lantern and joined O'Grady at the rear of the barn, where Ben and Jink were sitting on bales of hay alongside him.

"I don't suppose that introductions are necessary," O'Grady said.

"No," Gerald said.

He sneezed. He was sure he was going to be ill after his exposure to the wind and rain. His clothes were still wet, and they had rubbed him all the way home. His skin was going to be chafed raw.

He wiped his nose with a damp bandanna and looked at the three men seated across from him. The wavery light of the lantern cast shadows across their faces, and Gerald did not like the look of them at all.

Nevertheless, he spoke up firmly. "Now about the money," he said.

"Yes," O'Grady said. "About the money." He shook his head sadly. "It wasn't there, you see."

After Burt left, Ellie sat at the table for quite some time, staring out the door. She hardly noticed the lightning or the thunder, but when the rain began to fall she got up and walked out on the porch.

She watched the heavy drops spatter on the

ground, which was so hard that some of them bounced up and shattered into smaller droplets before soaking into the soil.

After the first scattered drops, when the rain began to gush from the sky, Ellie stepped off the porch and into the yard. She stood there rigidly for several minutes, and then she tore her garments from her, ripping her dress to shreds and stamping it into the mud under her feet.

She stood there nude, her eyes closed, her face to the sky, letting the water rush over her face, her bare arms, her naked breasts, her stomach and thighs.

After a while, she walked around to the back of the house, where there was a wash basin on a stand under a small overhang. Beside the basin was a bar of lye soap that Ellie had made herself.

She took the soap and scrubbed herself between the legs, scrubbing hard until she began to burn. She washed the soap away as best she could with the water from the basin and tossed the remaining water on the already drenched ground.

She walked in the rain back to the front of the house and sat on the edge of the porch while she cleaned the mud off her feet and ankles.

When she was completely clean, she went back into the house, water running off her naked body onto the wooden floor. Her hair was plastered to her face and neck, to her shoulders and breasts. Water steamed out of it and slid in rivulets down her back, stomach, and legs.

She twisted her hair and wrung the water out of it onto the floor. Then she got a towel and dried her hair vigorously. When she was satisfied with her hair, she dried all over. She threw the towel aside, got a dress, and put it on.

By then the rain had stopped and the sun was going down. Ellie lit a lamp and sat again at the table, staring out the door.

"Wasn't there?" Gerald said. "What do you mean, it wasn't there?"

"We mean it wasn't there, you fat sack of shit," Jink said. His finger was hurting like hell, and he didn't feel like putting up with Gerald Crossland. He wanted his money, and he wanted to get out of there.

O'Grady had counted the money soon after arriving at the barn, and Ben and Jink had been furious when they discovered that there was a little under twenty thousand dollars in the bag. They had calmed down a little, but not much.

"Yeah," Ben said to Gerald. "You said there'd be more than a hundred thousand in that there bank, easy. And look what we got."

He turned and pointed to the piles of money that were stacked on a bale of hay behind the one where O'Grady had been sitting. Gerald could see that the stacks were not very large, not nearly as large as they should have been.

Gerald could feel his face getting hot and red.

"You're trying to cheat me," he said. "You're trying to cheat me out of my fair share of the money."

O'Grady was the only one who seemed unruffled. "No one is trying to cheat you," he said. "If anyone has been cheated, sure and it's us. But maybe you have an explanation."

"No," Gerald said. "There's no explanation. What you're saying is impossible. The money was there. I know it was. It had to be there."

"I can regretfully assure you that it wasn't," O'Grady said. "I looked most carefully. What you see there is all there was, believe me."

"I *don't* believe you. You're lying, but you won't get my money. I'll—"

Gerald didn't get to say what he might do. Jink got up from the hay bale, drawing his pistol as he did so. He stepped over to Gerald and rammed the barrel of the gun into Gerald's large, soft belly.

"Uffff," Gerald said, doubling over and taking two steps backward.

Jink was about to club him in the back of the head with the pistol butt when O'Grady said, "No."

Jink looked back over his shoulder, the pistol butt still poised above Gerald's head. Gerald remained bent over, sucking wind and afraid to move.

"Why the hell not?" Jink said.

"It won't get us the money," O'Grady said.

"I don't think there ever was any money," Ben said. "This lyin' son of a bitch never intended for us to get it."

"Yes I did," Gerald said. He had gotten his breath back and straightened up, though he still kept a wary eye on Jink, who had not holstered the pistol. "You don't think I asked you to rob the bank for some kind of stupid joke, do you?"

"We aren't really in the way of knowing why you asked me," O'Grady said. "Considering that the money you mentioned wasn't there."

Gerald clenched his fists and closed his eyes tightly as if he were in pain. "The old bastard," he said. "The conniving old bastard."

"Who you callin' a bastard," Ben said. Like Jink, he had drawn his pistol and was pointing it at Gerald.

"Not you," Gerald said. "I'm talking about my father. My goddamn father."

Rawls Dawson was ready to give it up. The hastily assembled posse had been ready to go home for an hour, but Dawson had kept them pressing on.

He hated to admit that there was really no chance of catching the robbers, but the rain had wiped out any trail that they might have left, the men in the posse were tired and discouraged, and it was clear by now that they were really just wandering aimlessly, hoping by some remarkable stroke of luck simply to happen on the robbers, who were probably not anywhere within ten miles of where the posse was looking for them. If they were smart, they were well on the way to Mexico by now.

Dawson was fifty years old, a sinewy man with a lined, weathered face and a great deal of determination that he'd never really had to use in the pursuit of criminals before.

Although he had been the town marshal in Blanco for ten years, for most of that time the worst thing that had ever happened was that someone would get drunk and bust up the White Dog Saloon, along with a couple of the men drinking there. Dawson would quietly arrest them and put them in the town jail, letting them go the next morning if they could pay their small fine. Sometimes, if they were really drunk, they would put up some resistance, but not enough so that Dawson would have to draw his gun. That was the way it usually went.

There had been only two killings in that whole time, and they weren't the kind to surprise anybody.

Esther Thomas had chopped her husband up with an ax one hot Sunday night a few years back, but everybody in Blanco knew that Zed Thomas was the kind of a man who needed chopping up. He beat his wife, and he beat his animals. If Esther hadn't killed him, one of his mules would probably have kicked him to death as soon as it got a chance when Zed wasn't looking.

And the first year that Dawson had been on the job, Harve Addison had shot his brother, Jack, in an argument over who had the best corn crop that year. Harve and Jack stayed drunk a lot of the time, and they'd been drunk then. After he sobered up, Harve didn't even remember what he'd done.

There'd never been any robberies in Blanco, either, not like the one at the bank. Just kids, pilfering candy at Rogers' Mercantile, or maybe somebody getting drunk and trying to stick up the bartender at the White Dog, using an unloaded pistol, as likely as not.

Dawson could deal with things like that. That was what he understood his job to be about. But he had always liked to think he could deal with bigger things as well, if bigger things ever occurred. In fact, he had often thought that if the occasion arose he would prove to the town that he could handle a major crime as well as anyone.

But it looked as if he were about to be proved wrong. For the first time, Blanco had experienced two real murders and a real robbery in the same day. And the livery stable had burned down. Dawson was pretty sure that the fire was connected to the other things, but he didn't have any proof.

He didn't have any proof of anything, and the killers had eluded him completely.

His horse topped a slight rise, and Dawson reined the gelding to a halt. The moonlight was almost as bright as day, and the few trees cast sharp shadows on the wet ground. There was no sign of a trail, no sign of anyone fleeing guiltily with ill-gotten gains. No sign of anything.

Earl Whistler rode up beside Dawson. "We might

as well give it up, Marshal," he said. "We ain't never gonna catch up to 'em."

"We'll catch 'em," Dawson said. He might call off the hunt tonight, but he would not give up. "We'll catch 'em sooner or later."

Elmer Wiley joined them. The banker was no longer dressed in his business suit, but he sat his horse stiffly, and he looked uncomfortable in his high-crowned hat and slicker.

"It's not your fault, Rawls," he said. "I think you'd better turn this over to the Rangers and let them handle it from here on out."

Dawson didn't like the idea of letting the Rangers in on things, but he had to admit that Wiley was right. Dawson's job was to stay in and around Blanco. The Rangers could cover the whole state.

"I'll get in touch with them tomorrow," he said. "First thing."

"Tonight," Wiley said. "Send a telegram when we get back to town."

Dawson sighed. "Tonight, then," he said. "I'll do it." He turned in his saddle and called out, "All right, men, it looks like we ain't gonna do any good out here. Let's head on back to town."

The posse didn't waste any time following his suggestion.

Chapter 7

❖

Abner Stone helped Alma down from the wagon. He had stopped as close to the Taines' porch as he could so her shoes would not get any muddier than necessary.

Alma picked up her skirts to take the two steps needed to reach the porch. She could see Ellie sitting at the table in the lamplight.

"Come along, Abner," she said, and her husband joined her after tying the horse to the hitching rail at the end of the porch.

They stood together in the doorway looking in at Ellie, who did not acknowledge their presence. It was as if they were invisible.

The Stones were not the kind to stand on ceremony, however, and they did not wait to be invited inside. Alma went in first and stood beside Ellie, putting her soft hand on Ellie's shoulder. Abner stood in front of them, on the other side of the table. If either

Alma or her husband was curious about the shotgun that lay in front of Ellie, neither of them said anything about it.

"I'm afraid we have some bad news, my dear," Abner said. "Something's happened to your husband."

Ellie raised her head slowly and looked at Abner Stone, as if noticing him for the first time. Stone couldn't remember ever having seen eyes so hard and cold.

"Burt?" she said. "What's happened?"

"He's been shot," Alma said, squeezing Ellie's shoulder.

Ellie felt the touch and remembered how she had spurned Burt's hand earlier. "How bad is he hurt?" she said.

"As bad as can be, I'm afraid," Abner said. He had found it best in such situations not to mince words. "He's dead."

Ellie's expression did not change. "Who shot him?"

"Bank robbers," Alma said. "Three men robbed the bank in town, and they shot Burt."

"Why?" Ellie said.

"No one knows for sure," Abner said. "Apparently he tried to stop them."

"Where is he?" Ellie said.

"He's at Mr. Fowler's," Alma told her.

Ellie shook off Alma's hand and stood up. "I'll need to hitch up the wagon."

"That's not necessary," Abner said. "We'll take

you into town. You can stay at our house tonight. You might not feel like coming back here."

"I might need the wagon," Ellie said.

"Very well," Abner said. "But I insist that you stay with us. I'll go hitch up your team, and you can follow us into town."

"You might want to bring Burt's Sunday clothes along," Alma said. "For the burying."

"All right," Ellie said. She went to fetch them.

Jonathan Crossland was not sleeping when Gerald entered his room this time, either, but again he pretended to be. He lay there, his arms resting atop the blanket that was pulled to his chin, his eyes closed, his breathing regular and slow.

The pain still ran through his veins like a river of fire, and he was convinced that he would not last the few more days that the doctor predicted, but he didn't want to share that fact with Gerald. No use to give him cause for rejoicing. Let him suffer a little, too.

"The old bastard looks all shriveled up," Jink said, looking through the doorway.

Obviously Gerald had company, which came as a surprise to Jonathan. He did not know that his son had any friends, and he did not recognize the voice.

"Maybe he's dead already," Ben said. "Damn sure looks like it."

Not yet, Jonathan thought. *But close enough.*

"He's not dead," Gerald said. "He's just asleep. He sleeps all the time."

Jonathan laughed inside himself at how easy Gerald was to fool. All a man had to do was lie there with his eyes closed, and Gerald thought he was asleep.

"Perhaps we should wake him up, then," O'Grady said. "And see what he has to tell us."

He walked over to the bed and looked down at the old man's face. It was creased and leathery, covered with a week's worth of bristly whiskers. His eyelids seemed so thin that O'Grady imagined he could almost see the eyeballs underneath them, and his lips were so pale that they were almost white.

O'Grady almost hated to wake the old man, but he put his hand on Jonathan's shoulder and shook him gently.

Jonathan tried to keep his eyes closed, but even the small movement that O'Grady had caused sent fresh spasms of pain shooting through him.

He jerked on the bed and raised his head slightly. "Juana?" he said.

"Who the hell is Juana?" Ben said.

"The woman who cooks for us," Gerald said. "She's not here today. I sent her to visit her daughter in Blanco. Here, let me talk to him."

He walked over to the bedside and looked at his father. It was hard to believe that the wasted old man lying there had at one time controlled half the rangeland around Blanco, had ridden from daylight to dark on the old cattle trails, had faced down his enemies and bested most of them.

"Juana?" Jonathan said again.

He knew very well that Juana was nowhere around, but he'd be damned if he was going to let on that he had any idea what was happening, especially since he really didn't know. Maybe if he could keep his mouth shut, Gerald would tell him.

"It's Gerald," his son said. "Juana isn't here today."

Jonathan moaned. He didn't have to fake that. He would have liked to scream aloud, but he bit down hard, snapping his teeth together.

"He tryin' to bite somethin'?" Ben said.

"He does that sometimes," Gerald said.

"Ask him about the money," O'Grady said.

"All right," Gerald said. "Father, something's happened to your money. Did you know that?"

"Money?" Jonathan moaned. "What money?"

"The money that you keep in the bank in town," Gerald said. "*That* money. Something's happened to it. Can you tell us about it?"

"Money?" Jonathan said.

"Goddammit," Jink said. "The old son of a bitch is out of his head. He ain't gonna tell us a thing. He don't even know we're here. I say we kill him and take what we can find in the house. Then we get out of here."

"I think we oughta eat, too," Ben said. His disappointment at hearing that the cook wasn't there was almost as great as his disappointment at finding that the money they had stolen was so much less than they had expected.

"Killing him would be doing him a favor," O'Grady said.

Right you are, son, Jonathan thought, suppressing another moan.

"And killing him won't help us find out about the money, either," Gerald said, trying to keep them thinking about what was most important.

"How do we know that you didn't fiddle the money out of the bank some way or other?" Jink said. "And then leave us to take the blame when we robbed it."

"I think you're giving Gerald credit for a bit too much imagination," O'Grady said. "I don't think he would do anything like that."

He sure as hell would, Jonathan thought, almost smiling now that he had some idea of what had transpired. He hadn't felt quite so happy for days. Weeks, probably. It was pretty damn funny.

He knew just how much imagination Gerald had, and that was why he'd had his money transferred to an Austin bank right after he'd found out how sick he was. He'd suspected that Gerald would try some way of getting his hands on the money, and he'd taken precautions. He hadn't bothered to mention them to Gerald, however.

Of course, he'd never dreamed that Gerald would get himself involved with bank robbers, but now that he realized what had happened, he wasn't really too surprised. Gerald might have imagination, but he'd always been lazy as an old yellow hound. He'd do anything to avoid working himself. What would be more natural than for him to find someone to do the work for him and take all the risks?

Jonathan felt a laugh rising up all the way from his stomach, and he opened his mouth to let it out.

But what came out was not a laugh.

It was a scream.

Ellie didn't sleep at all that night.

The bed was comfortable enough, much softer than her and Burt's bed back at the house. The sheets were clean, and ironed crisp.

But all Ellie could do was think about Burt.

They had taken her by to see him at Fowler's, but the thing she saw there didn't really look like her husband. He was covered to the chin by a thin sheet. Later, Mr. Fowler would dress him in the suit she had brought, but Ellie didn't think that would help.

There really hadn't been much Mr. Fowler could do about his face and head.

"Do they know who did it yet?" she said.

Fowler, a genial man when he was not doing his job, was also a man who liked to talk. He was not merely Blanco's undertaker; he was also one of the chief sources of information about what was going on in town.

"Just that it was the bank robbers," he said. "No one knows who they are, but there were three of them."

"What did they look like?"

"No one got much of a look at them," Fowler said. "Except for the people in the bank. They had their neckerchiefs pulled up over their faces, however."

"But the people in the bank must've seen something."

"Not enough. One of the men was big, and maybe had a beard. The one who gave the orders sounded Irish."

"What about the third one?"

"Skinny as a rake," Fowler said.

Ellie looked down at Burt. "I thought so," she said.

Fowler didn't ask what she meant by that.

Ellie stared dry-eyed at the bare ceiling of the bedroom where she lay. The moonlight came in through the windows, and a light breeze played with the curtains, but Ellie did not notice those things.

She was seeing into the past.

She remembered the day she and Burt had been married. It had not been a fancy wedding, just a quick ceremony in the minister's parlor, but it was enough for Ellie.

She had never really thought she would ever marry anyone. She was already twenty-five, and most women she knew had been married for years by that age.

She knew that there were some men who didn't like her because she wasn't at all pretty, not in the soft way that some women were. She could look in any mirror and see that easily enough.

But there was more to it than that.

There was something else about her that men didn't seem to like, an independent streak, her parents had called it. She wasn't one to sit back and let someone else take charge of her life, tell her what to do. She had a mind of her own, and it was filled with her own ideas.

By the time Burt Taine came along and showed an interest in her, she was resigned to spinsterhood, and she thought it wouldn't be so bad. You could do what you wanted to do, and there was no one to order you around, no one you had to satisfy but yourself.

She made a little money by sewing, and she had a good-sized garden in back of the house where she lived with her parents. She sold fresh vegetables, and then she bought some hens and started selling the eggs. When she had enough money, she bought a cow and started selling milk and cream. It was her intention to buy a small farm of her own when she had saved the cash she needed.

Her parents died of a fever that went around one winter. Ellie nursed them, trying to pull them through, but without success. After their deaths, she lived alone for two years, keeping house, sewing, gardening, doing the milking, gathering the eggs.

Burt Taine had grown up in Blanco, just like Ellie, and he was clerking at Rogers' Mercantile. None of the girls in town regarded him as much of a catch. They knew that Alf Rogers, Junior, would inherit the store, and they believed that Burt would remain a clerk there for the rest of his life, drawing a clerk's meager wages. So although he had kept company with one or two of the girls when they were young, they all found someone else when the time came for marrying.

That was when Burt noticed Ellie, as if for the first time, and it seemed that he settled on her from that moment. None of the other girls had known that Burt had a secret ambition, and certainly they would never have guessed that it was the same as Ellie's.

Not long after the two of them married, they bought the farm with money they had both saved.

And it hadn't been a bad life, Ellie thought. Burt might not have been the most romantic man in the world, but he seemed to care about her. He treated her as an equal on the farm, and she shared in all the decisions. They were making a go of it, and if there was anything lacking in their lives, Burt had never complained.

But then neither had she. She was a worker, not a complainer, and she had always believed that was one of the things Burt had seen in her.

What had she seen in him?

She had seen a man who had taken the trouble to

look beyond her admittedly homely face and see that there was something valuable there, something to be appreciated and maybe even loved, though she did not ever recall hearing him use that particular word.

She had never used it, either.

And if at the end he had died because of what he believed to be an insult to his own honor rather than hers, which she suspected was the case, that didn't really change anything. He was gone, and she was alone again.

Everything that they had worked for had been destroyed in the course of one day.

The rape had been bad enough, but she had begun to reconcile herself to that. She had been violated, but she was starting to realize that the violation of her body had in no way changed who she was.

She had cleansed herself in the rain, washing away the smell of the two men, washing away the touch of their hands on her flesh, and the cleansing of her body had begun the cleansing of her spirit, though the process was not yet complete. It might not be complete for a long time.

She had not been able to wash away the pain, of course, but that would fade. It was fading now. Though she still felt it between her legs, she knew that within a few days it would be gone.

What would not be gone was the memory of what the men had done to her, but she had thought that even that would fade. It would never go away, she knew that, but still it would fade, especially after the men who raped her were dead.

She supposed she believed that Burt would kill them somehow. He had looked so determined.

But they had killed Burt instead. She did not have the slightest doubt that they were the ones who had. There might have been three men involved in the robbery of the bank, but that made no difference at all. Two of them had been the men who raped her.

And then they had shot Burt, whose death had brought her a pain and a memory that would never fade.

She knew that the Stones must think that she was very coldhearted for her lack of tears, but she had no tears to cry. Crying was not her way.

Doing things, that was her way, thinking through a problem and finding a solution to it, then putting the solution into action. It was the same with a stump that needed grubbing out of a field or a cow that was having trouble calving.

It was the same now, though no one realized that except Ellie.

No one knew what she was planning to do tomorrow, as soon as Burt was buried in the little cemetery just outside of town.

No one knew that she had brought more than just Burt's Sunday suit to town.

She had put something else in the wagon while Alma Stone was helping to tidy up the house for Ellie's departure, and it was outside now, wrapped in a blanket under the wagon seat.

The shotgun.

It might not be possible now to wipe out the memory of what had happened, or ever to ease the pain of the loss she felt so strongly, but she was going to try.

She did not care that the men had robbed the bank. The bank meant nothing to her.

But they had violated her and they had killed Burt.

And she was going after them.

She was going to punish them for what they had done to her, but that was not the main thing. What mattered was that she was going to punish them for killing Burt.

She knew that he would have understood her motives, even if no one else would, and thinking of that, she was at last able to close her eyes and sleep.

Chapter 8

"Jesus, that old scutter scared the hell out of me, screaming like that," Jink said, stuffing his mouth full of scrambled eggs, the only dish besides bacon that Gerald knew how to prepare. "You reckon he's dead?"

"Naw, he just passed out," Ben said. "And you better hope to hell he ain't dead. Else he won't be able to tell us where the money's hid."

They were sitting at the rough wooden table in the kitchen of the ranch house, where Gerald had been more or less compelled to feed them. The bacon was too crisp, almost burned, and the eggs were too runny, but no one was complaining. They were all too hungry.

"I'm not sure he knows what happened to the money," Gerald said. "He's not really in his right mind."

He was glad that he had at least been able to convince the others that the money did indeed exist. He had been afraid that they might decide to take out their frustrations at its absence by doing something to him.

"Look at this house," he'd said. "Do you have any idea how much it cost? Think about that barn you were in. Think about the land that you rode through to get here. All of it's his, for miles around. There's money, all right. Or there was."

They had come to see it Gerald's way, but they were as puzzled as he was about where it could have gone. They knew for damn sure that it wasn't in the bank.

"I bet that old man knows," Jink said, crunching bacon as he talked. "I bet he's got it hid right here on this place somewheres."

O'Grady didn't really believe that the money was hidden on the ranch, and he had a funny feeling that the old man, though obviously quite ill, was not only aware of what was going on but was probably a lot smarter than even his son was willing to give him credit for being. The money was most likely stashed away in some safe place known only to him, or maybe even deposited in some other bank.

If that was the case, there wouldn't be any use looking for it. At the same time, however, O'Grady didn't want to take the chance that the money might be right there under their noses and just ride off without making some kind of search.

"What's your opinion of the matter?" he asked

Gerald, who was now making a pot of coffee. "Do you think there's a chance that the money is here?"

The coffee was ready, and Gerald poured it into thick crockery mugs. He didn't really know what to think about the money. If his father really was out of his mind, as he appeared to be, then it was possible that he had drawn the money out of the bank and hidden it somewhere on the ranch, though that would not have been like Jonathan at all. Or not like him before he got sick. Who could say what he might have become after that?

"It could be here," was all he said.

"Then we'll just have to find it," Ben said.

O'Grady didn't like the idea, but he didn't speak against it.

"We can stay here for the night," he said. "They'll more than likely be thinking we rode straight on out of the area, and they won't be looking for us around here. If we stay out of sight, we should be all right." He blew on the scalding coffee and then took a sip. "To-morrow we can look for the money, starting at first light. If we don't find it by noon, I'll be taking my share of the swag and riding on."

Ben and Jink agreed that O'Grady's idea was a good one. While they had hoped for much more, the money they had taken in the robbery was still far more than they had ever hoped to have at one time.

Gerald started to ask what his share would be, but he wisely refrained. He would worry about that later.

———

The next day dawned bright and cloudless. The sun burned down on Blanco and dried up all traces of the previous day's rain. The ground remained softer than usual, however, and made the job of digging Burt Taine's grave easier than it would otherwise have been.

Earl Whistler was up early, surveying the ruin of his stable. He had a shovel with him, but it wasn't for digging a grave.

He stuck the point of the shovel into the mud and leaned on the handle, looking at the ruins of the stable. He'd gotten the horses he'd been boarding for others out safely, and his own nags had been out of harm's way in the corral around to the side of the stable. Nevertheless, he was pretty much permanently out of business.

He didn't really mind, not all that much, anyhow. He was seventy-odd years old, and it was time for him to retire. He didn't have much, but he had enough. He had lived a simple life, living in a little room in the front of the stable for the last ten years since the death of his wife. He had saved his money, and luckily he had never really believed in banks. The money was buried in three jars in back of the stable.

Or what was left of the stable. There wasn't much. The hay and straw had burned hot and fast, and the old wooden building had been consumed by the flames quicker than he would have thought. Nearly everyone in town had tried to help save it, but they never had a chance.

What kind of a man is it, Earl wondered, *that would burn down a man's stable just to cover up a bank robbery?* It had to be a man who didn't care much about other folks and what belonged to them, that was for sure.

Nothing of the stable was left standing except part of one wall, and most of that was burned so badly that it looked as if it would fall to ashes at a good kick. Ashes and charred wood were about all that was left of the place. There would be some burned saddles under there, and some blankets, but there wouldn't be any-thing left of them, either.

In the middle of the whole mess were the recog-nizable remains of a buggy and a wagon, part of their frames still standing on wheels that had not been quite destroyed by the fire. There was not enough left of either one to make salvage worthwhile.

Earl sighed, took off his battered hat, and wiped the top of his bald head, staring out over the heap of ashes. There were some birds singing off in the trees, but their song didn't make Earl feel any better.

A man works hard all his life, he thought, *and this is what it comes to.* He jammed his hat back down on his head and walked around to what had been the back of the stable.

Now where the heck did I bury that jar? he won-dered. It had been easy enough to find when the stable had been standing. The stable had given him a point of reference.

Ten paces out from the tenth board on the back end,

he remembered. But how was he supposed to know where that tenth board had been?

He sighed again. There was no way to be sure. He'd just have to guess at it.

He could tell about where the wall used to be, so he estimated the width of the boards and when he got to where he thought the tenth one should have been, he took ten paces away from the burned structure.

Should be right about here, he thought. He looked down at where he was about to dig. There was something on the ground, and Earl bent down to pick it up.

It was what was left of a cigar. The rain had soaked it nearly to shapelessness, but Earl could tell what it was.

What the heck was a cigar doing there? he wondered. He didn't smoke cigars, didn't know hardly anybody who did, much less in back of the livery stable.

That was when he thought about Gerald Crossland. Crossland smoked cigars; Earl had seen him with one a time or two. And Crossland had come up and shaken Earl just before the fire started. Hell, it wasn't *before* the fire had started. The fire was already blazing. And Crossland had come into town a roundabout way if he'd wound up at the stable.

Earl decided that as soon as he'd dug up his money and taken it to the hotel room where he was staying for the time being, he'd look for Marshal Dawson and tell him about the cigar.

Maybe it didn't mean a thing.

But then again, maybe it did.

———

Burt Taine's funeral didn't last long.

The mourners, and there were quite a few of them, sang "Amazing Grace." Abner Stone read the twenty-third psalm and said the usual soothing things about the goodness of Burt's life on earth and the joy of the life eternal that a fine man like Burt could expect in the heavenly kingdom. After that, there was a prayer, and then the people stopped by to say whatever they could think of to Ellie before going back to their ordinary pursuits.

Ellie did not intend to stay to watch the grave filled. She wanted to get on her way, but she would have to go back to the Stones' house first to change from her dress into the blouse and riding skirt that she had brought along.

She had no idea where she was going; she simply knew that she was leaving. She had a general idea of which way the robbers had gone. She'd gotten that much from Abner Stone. She would start in that direction. She had a strong feeling that somehow or other she'd find the men she was looking for.

That feeling was confirmed just after Marshal Dawson came by to shake her hand and comfort her by telling her what a brave man Burt had been.

"If one man coulda stopped those scoundrels, Burt would've done it," he said.

Ellie nodded as if she agreed, but she said nothing. Dawson moved on, and as he did, Earl Whistler tugged at the sleeve of his shirt.

Ellie could hear them talking, and what they said was much more interesting that the conventional condolences that were being whispered to her.

"Gerald Crossland?" Dawson said. "You don't really think he had anything to do with it, do you? Anybody can smoke a cigar, Earl."

"All I know is, he was there when the fire started," Earl said, "and there was a cigar in back of where the stable used to be."

"Well, I guess I could look into it," Dawson said, thinking that he might as well. It would be something to do. Since he had sent the telegram to the Ranger station the previous night, there was really nothing else he was needed for. The Rangers would be looking for the robbers, and they were a lot better equipped for finding them than Dawson was. They were probably out of his jurisdiction by now anyway.

Ellie was more interested in Earl's speculations than Dawson had been. She had a place to begin looking now, and she could hardly wait for the consolations to end so that she could get started.

O'Grady had slept in Crossland's barn, along with Ben and Jink. They planned to be up early to begin their search.

Ben and O'Grady were up and ready to go, but there was something wrong with Jink.

His face was flushed and feverish. "It's my damn hand," he said, holding it up for them to see.

He had taken off the bandage, and his hand wasn't a pretty sight. The whole hand was swollen, but the finger that the woman had bitten after he cut it on the can lid was the worst part of it. It was half again its normal size, the skin stretched to the bursting point. The skin was so black that it was almost purple over most of the finger, though it was an angry red along the edges of the cut. The black was spreading down the finger and onto the back of Jink's hand.

"Goddamn," Ben said, looking at it.

O'Grady leaned down for a closer look. "Sweet Jesus," he said. "And what did you do to yourself, Jink, my lad?" He remembered what Jink had told him in the saloon. "A cut, you said?"

"Yeah. I cut it on a can," Jink said, thinking it best not to mention anything more of the circumstances.

Ben shook his head. "It's done mortified," he said.

Jink's beady eyes widened. "It's just a little cut, goddammit. I got some salve in my saddlebags. I'll put some of that on it."

O'Grady thought it was a little late for salve. "We should open it," he said. "Let some of the poison out."

Jink sat on a hay bale, gripping his hand by the wrist and holding it between his legs.

"Shit," he said. "That'll hurt."

"It hurts already, now doesn't it?" O'Grady said.

"You're damn right, it hurts," Jink said. "It hurts like hell. Jesus, what causes something like this?"

"Infection," O'Grady said. "Blood poisoning, most likely."

He walked over to where his saddle hung on the side of a horse stall and looked around in his saddle-bags for a second before bringing out a leather scabbard. He pulled a large single-edged skinning knife from the scabbard.

Jink's eyes widened even farther. "Jesus," he said. "Oh Jesus."

O'Grady reached back into the saddlebags and brought out a bottle of whiskey wrapped in a piece of an old blanket.

"Sure and it's a shame to waste good whiskey like this," he said. "But I suppose it has to be done."

He pulled the cork from the bottle with his teeth and poured whiskey over the knife blade. Then he replaced the cork and set the bottle on a hay bale.

"You gonna cut off his finger?" Ben said, able to stand the thought of Jink's pain fairly easily.

"No," O'Grady said. "Just lance it. You can help me."

The two of them walked over to Jink.

"You hold his hand down on the hay bale," O'Grady said.

"I don't need nobody to hold me down," Jink said.

"Just the same, I'd like Ben's help," O'Grady told him. "Go ahead, Ben."

Ben gripped Jink's arm and pressed down.

O'Grady touched the blade of the knife to the finger.

Jink screamed and tried to jerk his arm away from Ben, but Ben held it firmly.

"Oh, shit!" Jink said. "Oh, shit."

O'Grady cut the finger and greenish-yellow pus burst from it, spattering on the hay bale. It continued to ooze from the cut, but Jink didn't notice.

He didn't even feel it when O'Grady poured whiskey in the cut.

He had passed out.

Chapter 9

———◆—✦—◆———

Jonathan had actually slept for most of the night.

It had not been a restful sleep, but it had been sleep, and that was a vast improvement over his recent inability to escape from consciousness at all.

Maybe he should have screamed sooner, let out some of his pain and frustration, but he wasn't convinced that his outburst was what had allowed him to sleep. Besides, he hadn't screamed on purpose. The scream had escaped him when he was trying to laugh.

To tell the truth, he was a little ashamed of himself. A man just didn't give in to his pain like that, not for any reason.

All the same, he found that he felt better than he had for days. The pain was still there, all right, but it wasn't hurting him like it had been. It was as if it had receded somewhere into the background. He felt almost like getting out of the bed and eating breakfast.

That would be a real change. He hadn't eaten anything other than soup for nearly a month. Soup and crackers, for most of that time, until it had gotten to the point that he couldn't stomach the crackers. After that, it had been just the soup. He was damn tired of it, but it was all he could keep down.

But now for some reason he found himself craving bacon and eggs. He wondered where Juana was.

Then he remembered Gerald and his friends, if friends was the right word for them. Gerald had sent Juana away and brought in three desperados, three men who, apparently with Gerald's connivance, had robbed the bank in Blanco, hoping to get their hands on Jonathan's money.

They hadn't, thanks to Jonathan's foresight, but there was no telling what they might do now.

Jonathan turned his head and looked out the window. He figured that the sun had probably been up an hour. Maybe the men were no longer even there. Maybe they had left during the night.

They hadn't, however. He saw two of them coming out of the barn. He wondered where the third one was, and he wondered what they could be up to. Well, there was nothing he could do about it. His momentary good feeling would soon wear off, of that he was sure. About all he could do was pretend to be asleep as he usually did and hope that Gerald would come in and give him some clue about what was happening.

He lay there in the bed, and after a while, he could hear them rummaging about in the house. It occurred to him that they must be looking for the money, thinking that he'd hidden it somewhere around the ranch, as if he would be that stupid.

He wanted to laugh, but he didn't allow himself to give in to the impulse. He didn't want to scream again, not just yet.

They'd been looking for nearly an hour when Jink came into the house.

He didn't look any better than he had earlier, when they'd left him passed out in the barn. If anything, he looked worse. His shirt was sweated through, and his hair was lank and falling down in his eyes. His face was still red, and his eyes were watery. There was a clean bandage on his finger, but that had been put there by O'Grady.

"Where is it?" he said. "Where's the damn money?"

"Good Lord," Gerald Crossland said. "What's happened to him?"

"He cut his finger," O'Grady said.

"And we ain't found the money," Ben said for Jink's benefit.

"We better find it quick," Jink said. "I think I need a doctor."

Jink was right about the doctor, O'Grady knew, but he didn't really care. Whatever troubles Jink had, he had brought them on himself.

Jink was also right about their needing to find the money quickly. There was no telling who might come by. The cook might return, or someone from the town might just drop by to see how the old man was doing. If that happened, there might be trouble.

They had already ransacked most of the rooms, including the one that Jonathan Crossland had formerly used as an office. There was a wall safe in there, but it held nothing besides some papers that were of no value to anyone other than maybe the old man himself.

They were rapidly running out of places to look, and O'Grady was ready to leave off searching. It wasn't noon yet, but that didn't matter to O'Grady. He was ready to shake the dust of the ranch off his feet. He thought that he could avoid capture easily enough if he stayed away from the main trails and separated himself from Ben and Jink. The law would be looking for three men, not a lone rider.

"Is there any other likely place to be looking?" he asked Gerald.

Gerald couldn't think of one.

"What if the money ain't in the house?" Jink said. "What if he hid it outside? Shouldn't we look out there?"

"We can't be going around and digging up the entire ranch, now can we?" O'Grady said. "I think it's best that we split up the money now and go our separate ways."

"How much would the shares be?" Ben said, looking meaningfully at Gerald.

"Now that's what we'll have to be deciding,"

O'Grady said. "Why don't we go out in the barn and count the money once again."

"Sounds good to me," Ben said.

"Fine with me, too," Gerald said.

He could feel himself starting to sweat, but he wasn't going to let them go and count the money without him. They weren't going to cheat him out of his share. He couldn't let them do that. After all, it wasn't his fault there hadn't been as much money in the bank as there should have been. And if he hadn't burned the stable, they wouldn't have gotten away with as much as they had.

They trooped out to the barn. Ben sat on a bale of hay, but Jink seemed filled with a feverish, nervous energy. His eyes burned in his head, and he paced back and forth while O'Grady counted.

Gerald Crossland stood off to one side. He was glad they hadn't tried to stop him from coming with them. That must mean they were going to give him his share.

It took O'Grady a while to make the count. He did it slowly and carefully, wetting his thumb with his tongue as he separated the bills. He sorted the bills into stacks of different denominations, and he did the same with the gold coins.

When he was finished, he turned to them and said, "Nineteen thousand and thirty-one dollars."

"Shit," Jink said. "That sure ain't close to no hun'erd thousand."

"It comes out to almost five thousand a man, though," Gerald said. "That's not so bad."

It certainly wasn't as much as he'd hoped for, far from it. He would never be able to live the way he had planned, and the good life he had envisioned for himself was going to remain out of his reach. Nevertheless, five thousand dollars would get him by for a long time if he was careful. He might even be able to avoid having to get a job.

"Actually, it comes out to a little more than six thousand a man," O'Grady said.

"I don't see how you arrived at that figure," Gerald said, though he was afraid that he did see.

"I ain't much at cipherin'," Ben said, "but I can tell you how he came up with it. It don't include you."

"But that's completely unfair," Gerald said. He went on to point out his contribution to the robbery's success. "And you wouldn't ever have thought of it on your own," he added. "You wouldn't have anything if it weren't for me."

"That may be true," O'Grady said. "But who's to know? We might have come up with the idea of robbing some backwater bank all by ourselves." He looked at the money stacked neatly on the hay bale. "We could have gotten this much at any number of places. We didn't have to come to Blanco."

"But I helped you," Gerald said. "I burned the stable. I took a risk. I demand a share of the money."

"Shit on that," Jink said.

His pistol appeared in his hand, and there was an

audible click as he cocked the hammer with his thumb.

"Wait," O'Grady said, turning at the sound of hoofbeats and looking out the barn door. "Who's that?"

Someone had ridden into the ranch-house yard.

Ellie changed her clothing quickly and looked around the room.

Mr. Fowler had brought her the clothes that Burt had been wearing when he was killed, but Ellie didn't want them. She didn't want the boots, either. She decided to leave them in the room. There might be someone in town who could use them; the Stones would know if that was true.

There were two things, however, that she did want: Burt's pistol and gunbelt.

She took the pistol and held it in both hands. Burt had taught her how to use it, though she knew that she was not a very good shot.

The pistol was heavier than she remembered, but that didn't bother her. She slid it back in the holster and strapped on the gunbelt. It sagged down on her hips, putting the gun butt too low for an easy draw, but then she did not expect to be involved in a shoot-out. She would be able to get the pistol when the time came.

She walked out of the house and to the small barn

in back. She was accustomed to hitching the mules, and it did not take her long to get the team in harness.

She climbed into the wagon seat and turned to check that the shotgun was still there. It was, wrapped in the blanket with a box of shells.

Ellie was sorry to be slipping away without a word of thanks to the Stones, but she knew they would be curious about her rush to leave and about her clothing, and she didn't want to have to make up an explanation.

They would also be curious about the pistol, another item she would prefer not to talk about. When she got back to town, if she ever did, she would stop by and thank them for their kindness. Right now, she had other things to do.

She clucked to the mules and drove the wagon out of the barn.

It was a pretty day, with a clear blue sky, and the rain had cooled things down some. Marshal Rawls Dawson almost enjoyed his ride out to the Crossland ranch, and he felt a twinge of guilt about not having ridden out sooner. He had known Jonathan Crossland for a good number of years, and he should have paid a call on the old man before now.

That would be his excuse for showing up at the ranch, he decided. He felt a little strange about making a special trip to question Gerald Crossland about the burning of Whistler's stable. It didn't seem to

Dawson like the kind of thing that Gerald would be involved in. Why would Gerald want to help rob a bank? When Jonathan died, Gerald would probably *own* the bank.

Nevertheless, he felt he had to check things out, just in case there was some connection that he couldn't see. He could say that he was just dropping by to see how his old friend Jonathan was doing, not that it was any secret in Blanco that Jonathan was just about as good as in his grave.

The more he thought about it, the more Dawson realized that he actually did want to see Jonathan. He missed the old man, who had always stopped by the jail for a chat when he was in town. He had been a friend to everyone in town, unlike his son, who appeared to think he was better than everyone else, for some reason that Dawson couldn't make out.

The truth was that Gerald was about as sorry as owl shit, as far as anyone could tell. Besides being unfriendly, he was lazy, never having done a day's work in his life that anyone knew about.

There were times Dawson wished that he had married and had kids, and there were other times that he was glad that he hadn't. What if one of them had grown up to be like Gerald Crossland? Dawson didn't think he would have liked that at all.

The gate to the fenced ranch yard was open, so Dawson rode on through. He stopped his horse and looked around the yard. It wasn't as well kept as it had once been, but Dawson wasn't surprised. He'd heard that Jonathan Crossland had let all his hands go, and Gerald damn sure wouldn't be the kind to do any work around the place, no matter what it looked like.

Dawson climbed down from his horse and flipped the reins over the hitch rail. "Hello, the house," he called.

"It's the marshal," Gerald said, with feeling of considerable relief. He might not get a share of the loot from the robbery, and he might even go to jail, but Jink probably wouldn't kill him right there in front of the marshal.

However, it was hard to tell about someone like Jink, who was looking crazier by the minute.

Gerald decided that it would be for the best if he got out of the barn.

"I'm over here, Marshal," he said in response to Dawson's call, and as soon as he said it, he started outside.

"You son of a bitch," Jink said. He shot Gerald in the back.

The echo of the shot bounced around the barn, and before it had died, Ben had drawn his own pistol and was firing it at Gerald, who continued out of the barn, running now as fast as he could.

O'Grady stared at them in amazement. Maybe Jink had some excuse; he was sick. Or maybe just crazy. But Ben? Why was Ben shooting? Didn't he have any sense at all?

Gerald was fat, but surprisingly graceful as he ran. Not only did his fat not prevent him from running, it also kept him alive longer than anyone would have thought.

He could feel the bullets strike him, but they didn't hurt the way he thought they would. They threw him off stride, but that was all.

He was going to make it to the marshal, and Dawson would take care of him.

Then everything would be all right.

Chapter 10

❉

Dawson didn't know what the hell was going on.

He saw Gerald Crossland running out of the barn, and he heard the shots, but at first he didn't know whether they were being fired at him or at Gerald.

Then he saw Gerald stagger and knew that Crossland had been hit. He drew his own pistol and started toward him.

"Marshal!" Gerald called. "Help!"

Two slugs slammed into Gerald at one time, both of them striking him just below his left shoulder blade, and it was as if he had been kicked by a mule. He pitched forward in the mud and slid on his stomach for four or five feet.

For a second, he didn't even realize that he had fallen. His feet kept moving as if he were still trying to run.

He looked up and saw Marshal Dawson heading toward him. The marshal was firing into the barn.

"It's the men from the bank," Gerald said. His voice was not much more than a whisper. "They tried to rob me, too."

He was glad to see the marshal. He knew that he had been in real danger for a while there, but now that the marshal was here, Gerald thought, everything would be fine.

That was the last thought Gerald ever had.

His breath went out of him in a rush, and the world turned black as night. His feet twitched one last time; then his neck went limp. As Dawson ran past him, his face splatted into the mud.

O'Grady didn't waste any more time on Ben and Jink. As far as he was concerned, their partnership was over. He couldn't be partners with crazy men.

He swept the money off the hay and into the bag he had carried it from the bank in. He tied the top of the bag and threw a saddle his horse. By the time Ben and Jink caught on to what he was doing, he was riding hell-bent past them and out the barn door.

O'Grady put his heels to the horse's flanks and whipped the reins from one side of its neck to the other, riding straight at the marshal.

Dawson got off one shot before he threw himself to the side. O'Grady's horse cleared Gerald's body and was already out the gate before Dawson got himself turned around to fire a futile shot after him.

"That son of a bitch O'Grady has our money!" Jink screamed. "We gotta get after him!"

Ben reloaded and started to saddle his horse while Jink fired out at the marshal, who was now firing back at them.

"Saddle mine, too," Jink said as he reloaded. "I can't do it with this damn hand."

Ben saddled Jink's horse and said, "Let's go."

Jink couldn't get hold of the saddle horn with his bad hand, but he managed to hook his elbow around it and get mounted.

"We gotta take care of that marshal," he said.

"Yeah," Ben said.

They rode out of the barn, guns blasting.

Dawson never had a chance.

Ben and Jink didn't manage to hit him with every shot, but they did more than sufficient damage, hitting him in the right shoulder, the left side, the belly, and the neck.

The stomach wound would have killed him eventually, but the bullet through his neck did it decisively and quickly. It sliced through a carotid artery, which sent jets of blood pumping out ten feet in front of Dawson before he fell.

As his knees buckled, Dawson put his hand to his throat to stop the bleeding, but Jink's horse crashed into him, knocking him backward and sending blood fountaining straight up into the air. Some of it spattered on Jink and the horse, and then they were past him and out of the yard.

They didn't look back. They were no longer interested in Dawson. They were looking for O'Grady.

Jonathan saw most of it through his window.

He pushed himself up when he heard the shots, and he saw Gerald running from the barn. He saw his son fall. He knew that Gerald must surely be dead, but the only sorrow he felt was for himself.

He was sorry that he couldn't find any grief anywhere inside him for his son.

Gerald was dead, but there was no sense of loss in Jonathan, none at all. There was just a sense of emptiness. It was as if Gerald had died a long time ago as far as Jonathan was concerned.

He saw the man hightail it out of the barn and try to ride down Rawls Dawson. He wondered for a second how the marshal had found out the men were there, and then he watched helplessly when the other two men came charging out of the barn and gunned Dawson down.

When they were gone, he lay back on the pillow breathing a little faster, but otherwise not too much affected by what had happened. When a man is so close to his own death that he can reach out and touch it, seeing other men die doesn't worry him overmuch.

After a while, Jonathan sat up in the bed. There were two men lying out there in his yard, and one of them was his son. He supposed he should do something about them.

He swung his legs over the side of the bed and stood up. He hadn't been out of the bed in weeks, and he nearly fell. He had to sit down on the side of the bed until his head stopped swimming.

It cleared up in a minute or so, and he stood again. This time he was all right.

The funny thing was that he felt almost good. Not like he ought to, but not nearly as bad as he had been feeling. The pain had continued to recede, and now it was more like a dull ache that lingered in every part of his body. It was nothing he couldn't put up with. He didn't even need to yell anymore.

His clothes were hanging on a chair, where they'd been since he took to the bed. He had refused to put them away. He wanted them right there where he could put them on in case he got up. He had never really expected to wear them again, but he put them on now, liking the way the worn jeans felt as they slid over his legs, the way the shirt touched him when he buttoned it.

The jeans were loose, but he took the belt up a couple of notches and decided they'd stay on. He put on a pair of socks and slid his feet into his boots. They still fit just fine.

He walked into the kitchen. He wasn't what you could call steady on his feet, but he got where he was going.

What he needed was some food, he thought.

Something to eat, and he'd be just fine again, ready to go out and do a day's work around the ranch. He didn't feel like fixing anything, however. He looked around until he found a can of beans and a can of sardines.

He opened the can of beans and ate a bite or two to see if he could keep them down. He could. They tasted better than anything he could ever remember eating, and he gobbled the rest of them right out of the can, following them with the oily sardines.

He was feeling even better by the time he finished, but he wasn't fooled by that.

He'd knew what was happening to him. He'd seen it happen to others.

Once, on a trail drive Jonathan had been on as a young man, a cowboy named Zach Chaney got in the way of a herd of stampeding cattle and had the bad luck to fall off his horse.

They'd run all over him, stepped on his legs, his hands, his arms, his stomach, even his head. Chaney was as busted up as any man Jonathan had ever seen, and the things you could see, like the arms and hands, weren't half as bad as the stuff you couldn't see. Chaney was busted up inside, too.

Everybody on the drive knew that Chaney was a goner, though nobody actually came out and said that to his face. They put him in the chuck wagon after they got the herd rounded back up, and they told him that they'd get him to a doc as soon as they came to a town.

They were three days from a town, though, and they knew Chaney would never make it that long.

He didn't, but he nearly fooled them.

For two days, he got steadily worse. By the end of the second day, he was feverish and out of his head, mumbling about things that meant nothing to anyone but himself. For a while, he seemed to think he was in some swimming hole with his brother, Jimmy, back when they were kids. Then he was apologizing to a schoolteacher for fighting in the classroom. He blabbered about some girl he'd known when he was four-teen.

The ones who heard him just shook their heads. They figured he wouldn't last the night.

But sometime toward morning his fever broke, and he woke up bright-eyed and eager, impatient to get back on his horse and ride with the herd.

They tried to talk him out of it, but he insisted that he was feeling fine, just fine, and there hadn't been much they could do to stop him, short of tying him up, and they didn't want to do that.

So he got out of the wagon and climbed up on his horse, with a little help. He rode drag most of the day. About three o'clock, somebody looked back and saw the horse coming along without a rider.

Jonathan had been the one who rode back to look for Chaney. He found him lying on the ground, right where he'd fallen from the saddle. He was covered with trail dust, but there seemed to be a smile on his face.

It wasn't such a bad way to go, Jonathan thought now, riding along and feeling like everything was going to be all right. One minute you were there, and the next you were gone. That was the way it ought to be, all right. A man ought not to have to die a little bit every day, lying flat on his back so that all he knew about the world was what he could see out some damn bedroom window.

Jonathan figured that he was in just about the same fix Chaney had been in. He wasn't really getting better; more likely, he was just about to die.

Well, that didn't much matter. He'd been expecting that for a good while.

What mattered was that it didn't look like he was going to have to die in the bed. He was going to be up on his feet, the way it should be.

Maybe. Or maybe he'd just get sick again and have to go lie down.

No, by God. He wasn't going to do that, whatever happened. No matter how bad the pain got, he wasn't going back to the bed. He was sorry he'd ever done it in the first place. He should've taken his pistol out behind the barn and shot himself in the head before he'd taken to his room, and that was what he'd do this time, for damn sure.

He went back into the bedroom. His holster was lying in the chair, and he strapped it on. The pistol was so heavy that it threatened to weight him down, but he didn't take it off. He wasn't going to be without it from now on. A man never knew when he might need it.

Jonathan patted the gun butt and walked out of the room. It was time to take care of Marshal Dawson.

And Gerald.

The wagon rattled along the muddy, rutted road, the mules twitching their ears or switching their tails at the occasional fly.

Ellie Taine had never been to Crossland's ranch, but she knew where it was. Everyone around Blanco knew that.

She also knew Jonathan and Gerald Crossland, or at least she knew who they were. It wasn't as if they were friends of hers. Jonathan had attended the Methodist church once or twice, and she had been introduced to him. One of the women at the church had told her that he was very sick, just about to die, and she was sorry to hear it. He seemed like a fine man.

She had seen Gerald in town at the mercantile store, but he clearly wasn't the same kind of man his father was. He didn't bother to speak to anyone, or even acknowledge that anyone was there. He seemed all wrapped up in himself, and Ellie didn't much like him.

She found it hard to believe that either one of the Crosslands would have anything to do with a bank robbery. They were rich men, the kind of men who had more money than Ellie could ever dream of, but she had learned that you never could tell about people and what they might do. Maybe there wasn't any such thing as having as much money as you needed. Maybe you'd always want a little more and do what you had to in order to get it, even if it meant robbing a bank and killing a man.

So she would start at the Crossland ranch. Anyway, she didn't have any choice other than to go there. At least it would be a starting place. Where would she have gone, after all, if she hadn't overheard what Earl Whistler had told the marshal? She had been determined to set off after Burt's killers, but how would she have known where to go? She would have been crazy just to go off looking wildly about the country, but she would have done it anyway.

She was a little amazed at her own resolve, considering what had happened to her only the day before—*funny*, she thought, *it seemed much longer ago than that*—but she was confident that nothing like that would happen again.

This time, she was prepared. This time, she had the shotgun. And the pistol.

She would not be a victim again.

She saw the ranch house ahead. It was low and long, and it was surrounded by a wood fence made of cedar posts and cedar boards. The gate was open, and there was a horse at the hitching rail.

Ellie was sure it must be the marshal's horse. She had hoped to get there ahead of him, but she had not been able to get away from the cemetery. She wondered if the marshal had been able to get anything out of Gerald Crossland or if he had actually been involved in the robbery at all.

Then she saw the bodies in the yard.

Chapter 11

✦━━❊━━✦

O'Grady rode hard and fast, pushing his big gelding to the limit. He knew that Ben and Jink wouldn't be far behind him, but he hoped they'd be slowed down by Jink's fever.

He also found himself hoping that the infection in Jink's finger was just as bad as it looked and that it would spread fast. If it did, O'Grady might not have to deal with both of them, because Jink would be dead.

He turned the horse into a narrow draw, came out near a little wood of oaks and pecans, and entered the trees. He thought he might have as much as a full day before anyone got on his trail, anyone except for Ben and Jink.

Gerald Crossland and the Marshal were both assuredly dead, and the old man didn't look as if he'd be riding into town for help. The Marshal would be missed eventually, but by the time that happened, and by the time his deputy could get a posse organized, O'Grady would be a long time gone.

He wished that Ben and Jink weren't so trigger-happy. Even killing a citizen in the course of a robbery, even killing Gerald Crossland, wasn't as bad as killing a marshal, which was a sure way to get every lawman in the state on your trail. You'd think they'd know that, but it was as if they didn't care. Or as if they didn't even give it a thought.

The marshal showed up at the wrong time, he was a threat, they shot him. That's all there was to it.

Of course O'Grady didn't have a thing to do with killing the marshal, or with killing Gerald Crossland or the teller or the man who'd been outside the bank.

But that didn't matter. He was in just as much trouble as Ben and Jink. He was sure that if the law ever caught up with him, they wouldn't be asking him how much shooting he'd done. If they did, they'd be asking him after he was shot full of lead himself.

It wasn't anything he was looking forward to, nor was he looking forward to seeing Ben and Jink again. They likely wouldn't take kindly to the fact that he'd run off with all the money.

He rode as fast as he could through the trees, putting up a hand to keep the branches from whipping his face. He'd be coming to the Blanco River soon, and maybe he could travel in the shallow water for a way and throw off his pursuers.

He'd decided to go back to Mexico. There were disadvantages to living there, it was true, but the money he had would last him a lifetime down south of the border. He would never have to resort to robbery again once he was in Mexico.

All he had to do was get there.

"Goddammit, how far ahead of us could he be?" Jink said. He and Ben were riding slowly, looking for some sign of O'Grady. "I don't see how we let him get out of our sight. You shoulda saddled the damn horses quicker."

Ben didn't answer. He was leaning down from the saddle, trying to follow that son of a bitch O'Grady's trail. Ben wasn't all that good a tracker, even when the ground was muddy and making things easy for him, and he wished Jink would just shut up.

But Jink wasn't about to be quiet. "I don't see why he ran out on us like that," he said. "We was just tryin' to take care of things the best way we could. That fat bastard would've got us all killed back there, killed or stuck back in prison, and I've had all of that prison I ever want."

Ben couldn't figure it out. Jink had never been much of a talker before, but now it was like he couldn't stop.

"How's your finger?" Ben said. Maybe that would keep him quiet.

Jink held up his hand and looked at it. It didn't look quite as bad as it had, and the swelling in the finger was going down. Just the same, he didn't feel any too pert.

"It's better now," he said. "I guess I oughta thank O'Grady when we catch up to him. Right before I shoot him."

"He turned down this draw," Ben said, reining his horse to a stop.

"You reckon he's waitin' for us at the other end?"

"Naw. He's too busy runnin'."

"I hope you're right," Jink said. "I don't want to go and get bushwhacked."

"O'Grady wouldn't do nothin' like that."

"The hell he wouldn't. He took our money and ran off with it, didn't he?"

Ben didn't say anything. He kneed his horse and started into the draw.

Jink hung back. A man who'd steal from you would just as soon bushwhack you too. If Ben wanted to ride into it, that was fine. But Jink wasn't that stupid.

When Ben rode out of the draw, Jink was a good way behind him. While he waited on Jink to catch up, he built himself a smoke and took a few puffs. He didn't enjoy it. He'd been looking forward to smoking store-bought ready rolls for the rest of his life, what with all the money he'd expected to get out of that damn bank.

When Jink caught up with him, Ben snapped away the cigarette and said, "Looks like he went into them trees over yonder."

"Damn," Jink said.

"Don't worry so much," Ben told him. "He's not gonna ambush you in there. He's gonna keep runnin'. We ain't the only ones after him."

Jink looked back over his shoulder.

"I didn't mean they was closin' in," Ben said. "But they'll be along."

"Then we better get to him before any damn posse does," Jink said. "I want my share of that money."

"We'll get him," Ben said. "He's gotta stop sooner or later."

"What about us?" Jink said.

"We're gonna keep goin'. We won't stop till we catch up to him."

Jink didn't know about that. There'd been a time when he could stay in the saddle for a day or so without rest and not be too broken down when the ride was over, but that had been a few years back.

And it had been when he was healthy. He didn't feel healthy now.

"What if we can't keep goin'?" he said.

"I can," Ben said.

Jink looked at his old buddy. "I guess you'd bring my share of the money back to me if I had to stop and rest, then."

"Sure I would. You know me, Jink."

"Yeah, I know you, all right," Jink said. "That's what's got me worried."

————

Jonathan took his flat-crowned black hat off the peg by the back door, settled it on his head, and went out into the yard. He still wasn't as certain on his feet as he would have liked, but he was managing all right.

The worst thing was the sunlight. He'd been cooped up in the house for so long, the light was a real bother to his old eyes.

As he went around the corner of the house, he heard a wagon coming into the yard, and he stopped. He didn't want to run into any friends of that bunch of killers.

He waited until the wagon came to a halt, and then he peeked around the house. There was a woman sitting in the wagon, looking down at the body of Rawls Dawson.

He thought he recognized the woman, but he didn't have any idea why Ellie Taine would be at his ranch. Well, there was one way to find out.

He stepped into the yard.

"Oh," Ellie said, when she saw him.

She turned and fumbled under the wagon seat, coming out with the shotgun in her hands. She pointed the gun at Jonathan and cocked both hammers.

"Stay where you are, Mr. Crossland," she said. She hardly recognized him. His face was gaunt and gray, covered with stubbly whiskers.

"Don't you worry, ma'am," Jonathan said. He touched the brim of his hat to her. "I ain't goin' nowhere."

"That's Marshal Dawson on the ground," Ellie said. "Is he dead?"

" 'Pears that way to me," Jonathan said. "I ain't had a chance to get a good look at him."

"Who's that over there?" she said, nodding toward Gerald's body.

Jonathan looked in that direction, too. "That's my boy," he said. "That's Gerald."

"Did they shoot each other?"

Jonathan shook his head. "No, ma'am, that ain't exactly what happened."

"Did you . . . ?"

"No, ma'am, I didn't have a thing to do with it. I would've saved 'em both if I could."

Ellie kept the shotgun pointed at him. It was quite heavy, but she didn't let the barrels waver.

"What happened then?" she said.

"There was three other men here," Jonathan told her. "Bank robbers, most likely."

"Those are the men I'm looking for," she said. "They killed my husband."

"I'm right sorry to hear that," Jonathan said. "Burt Taine was a good man."

"Your son—Gerald—did he have anything to do with the robbery?"

"Seems like he must have. I don't know the whole story. I ain't been up to snuff lately, so I don't know exactly what all's been goin' on around here. But I think Gerald was mixed up with those three. I surely do."

Jonathan felt a sudden wave of weakness surge through him. "I need to sit down for a minute," he said. "You wouldn't mind if I did that, would you?"

"No," Ellie said. She put the shotgun on the wagon seat. "What are we going to do about the Marshal and your son?"

Jonathan was already on his way back inside the house. "Why don't you come in, and we can talk about it," he said.

They sat at the kitchen table and drank well water from tin cups.

"That tastes mighty fine," Jonathan said, draining his cup and setting it on the wooden tabletop. "Sometimes you forget how good things can taste." He looked at Ellie. "Now, then, why don't you tell me what you meant when you said you were lookin' for those three men that robbed the bank."

"I told you," Ellie said. Her cup was still nearly full. "They killed my husband."

"That's the truth. You told me that. But that don't explain why you're looking for them."

Ellie didn't say anything.

Jonathan's eyes widened. "You don't mean to tell me that you're thinkin' to capture 'em," he said. "A woman, by herself, lookin' to find three desperadoes and put 'em behind bars?"

"I'm not looking to put them behind bars," Ellie said.

"Godamighty," Jonathan said, putting a skeletal hand to his forehead. "You can't mean you're gunnin' for 'em."

Ellie said, "Killing my husband wasn't all they did."

Jonathan looked at her across the table. Her mouth was tight, her eyes determined.

"What else did they do?"

Ellie had thought she would never tell anyone what had happened, not anyone except Burt, but she did. "They raped me," she said. "Two of them did."

"Godamighty."

"I'm going to find them," Ellie said. "And when I do, I'm going to kill them."

Jonathan didn't know what to say, but he felt that he had to say something.

"I don't want to discourage you, ma'am, but those are three real bad men. I expect Marshal Dawson thought he was man enough to stand up to 'em, but he's dead out there in my yard. Gerald, well, he wasn't much good for anything, and he took his bullets in the back, but that just shows you the kind of men they are. They're the kind that'd shoot a fella in the back while he was runnin' away from 'em."

"I don't care about that," Ellie said. "I'm going to find them. And when I do—"

"Yeah. I know," Jonathan said. "You're gonna kill 'em, I know. You said that already. But I still think it's gonna be a lot harder than you think it is."

"I guess I'll find that out, then," Ellie said. "When I find them."

"Yeah." Jonathan fiddled with his cup for a few seconds. Then he said, "I was wonderin' if, before you go off after 'em, you'd mind helpin' me with somethin'."

"What?"

"Well, I thought I was gonna be able to do it myself, but now I can see I ain't quite up to it. I was gonna bury my son."

"I'll help you," Ellie said.

She had never dug a grave before, and it was hard work, but Ellie was up to it. It took her a couple of hours, but she got down deep enough.

It was even harder to get Gerald's body into the wagon than it was to dig his grave. He must have weighed close to two hundred and fifty pounds, and his body gave new meaning to the phrase "dead weight."

Jonathan wasn't much help. He wanted to be, but he was simply too frail and too weak to be of much use.

Ellie finally got the body loaded into the back of the wagon. Gerald's legs dangled off the end, but that didn't bother Ellie any. She wasn't going to drag him any farther into the wagon.

She drove to where she'd dug the grave, a spot under a cottonwood tree on a little rise about a quarter

of a mile from the house, and Jonathan helped her pull
Gerald off the wagon bed.

Gerald was lying on his back, and he left long
streaks of blood on the wood when they slid him out.
He was too heavy for them to catch when he came out
of the wagon. They tried, but he hit the ground hard,
splattering mud.

"Don't matter none," Jonathan said. "He don't
need dignity now."

They rolled the body into the grave, and Ellie realized she was about to attend her second funeral of
the day.

It was even shorter than Burt's.

"There ain't no words," Jonathan said, removing
his hat. "He wasn't much, but he was my boy. I'm sorry
he had to die the way he did." He put his hat back on.
"Here, now. Let me help you shovel him over."

"I'll do it," Ellie said, digging the shovel into the
mounded dirt and pitching a load down on Gerald. He
had landed on his back, and he was looking up at her
with staring, sightless eyes. She covered his face first.

"What are you going to do about the marshal?"
she said as she worked.

"I been studyin' on that," Jonathan said. "I
thought maybe you could take him back to town, let
folks know what happened here. They could get up a
posse and go after them fellas."

"I'm not going back to town," Ellie said. She
paused for a minute to wipe her face. She had already

worked up a sweat, even though the tree provided a bit of shade. "I told you what I was going to do."

"I thought maybe you'd give up that idea," Jonathan said. "Don't seem to me like you've got much chance of findin' 'em. Ain't no tellin' where they've got to by this time."

"I'll find them," Ellie said, tossing in another shovelful of dirt on Gerald.

"Damn if I don't believe you," Jonathan said after a while. "Well, that don't help me none with the marshal."

"If you've got a wagon, I'll hook up your team for you," Ellie said. "You could take him back to town."

She didn't really think he'd make it, not the way he looked.

"I guess I could take him in, at that," he said. "I expect folks sure would be surprised to see me. But I got a better idea."

"What?" Ellie said.

"I think I'll just go along with you."

Ellie stopped shoveling. She stuck the blade of the shovel in the dirt and said, "I must not have heard you right."

"You heard me right. I said I was thinkin' about goin' along with you."

"You can't do that," Ellie said.

"Why not? They killed my boy, same as they killed your husband."

"I told you. They did more to me than just kill Burt."

"I know it."

"And besides that, you don't look too good. I heard in town that you were just about dead."

"Well, I guess I am," Jonathan said. "That's why I want to go."

Ellie looked at him questioningly.

"It's kinda hard to explain," he said.

Ellie started shoveling again. "You might as well try," she said.

There was a slight breeze blowing, and it rustled the leaves of the cottonwood tree. Jonathan looked around him. All the land he could see in any direction belonged to him. Once it had been populated with some of the best beef in Texas, but those days were gone now. There wouldn't be any more herds of cattle there, not that Jonathan would live to see, and there was no one to leave the land to, not even Gerald, who would just have let it go to tarnation anyhow.

Jonathan felt like a man who had outlived his usefulness and outlived his time. He would've been better off to've died like Zach Chaney, out there on the trail someplace, riding along with a herd, but that wasn't going to happen. He'd missed his chance at that.

But that didn't mean he'd have to die meekly in bed like some dude back East who'd never seen a cow and never slept outside under the full moon.

He could do one last thing. He could go looking for the men who killed his son, and if he didn't live long enough to find them, at least he'd die outdoors and not closed up under a roof and behind four walls.

He'd die while he was *doing* something, not while he was lying down as if he were just waiting for his life to end, and the sooner the better.

He tried to explain all of that to Ellie Taine, and when she finished covering the grave, she looked at him thoughtfully.

"You're sure that's really why you're wanting to go? You're sure it's not because I'm a woman, and you think somebody ought to take care of me?"

Jonathan smiled. It seemed to him that it was the first time he'd done that in a month of Sundays.

"I'm afraid it'd be the other way around," he said. "My days of takin' care of folks are over."

"I can't take care of you, either. And if you did go with me, I wouldn't want you to go dying on me while we're on the trail. I wouldn't have time to bury you."

"You wouldn't have to. Just leave me where I fall. I don't figure it'll matter much to me, one way or the other."

"If you got sick on me, I couldn't nurse you," Ellie said. "You'd just have to lie in the wagon and keep quiet."

"I'm pretty good at that," Jonathan said. "Keepin' quiet, I mean."

"What would we do with the marshal?" Ellie said.

"I guess we'd have to bury him," Jonathan said. "But not too deep."

Chapter 12

＋•＋ ▰▰ ＋•＋

O'Grady was tiring, but he knew he couldn't afford to stop. His horse was tired; too, but they'd both had a drink at the river. They could go for a while longer.

He'd come out of the woods near the river, and he'd walked the gelding along in the shallows for about a mile before he located a low-water crossing and went across.

When he reached the opposite bank, he turned right and rode for another mile, until he found a particularly rocky patch of ground. He rode into the rocks, then turned back and rode down into the shallow water by a slightly different route. He headed back the way he'd come from, riding until he'd passed well beyond the place where he'd crossed the river. Only then did he turn south again.

While he didn't hold out any real hope that his maneuvering would throw Ben and Jink completely off his trail, he thought maybe it would buy him some time.

He hadn't seen anything of them yet, but he knew they were back there. They wouldn't let the money slip away from them without a fight.

Unless that marshal had stopped them. Somehow, O'Grady didn't think that was very likely.

The country before him was hilly and rocky, covered with scrub brush and cedars. There wasn't much in the way of cover, except for the occasional taller cedar tree or good-sized rock, but at least he could try to keep the hills between himself and Ben and Jink.

He smiled and urged his horse to go just a bit faster. He was beginning to think he was going to make it.

Ben and Jink were indeed falling farther behind.

Jink was no better at tracking than Ben was, and O'Grady's gambit at the river did throw them off the track for a while. It took them more than half an hour to figure out where they'd gone wrong, and then it took them another half hour to pick up the right trail.

Jink blamed it all on Ben, who, according to Jink, had taken too long to saddle the horses, lost the trail in the first place, and was generally useless when it came to tracking a man through the woods.

"I found the damn place where he came out of the woods," Ben said. "If you wanta take over, go ahead. Right now."

But Jink couldn't take over. He was feeling a little dizzy, a condition he attributed to the sun, which hadn't ducked behind a single damn cloud all day as far as Jink could remember. Anyway, he couldn't lean down and do any tracking from the saddle, and he was damn sure he couldn't do any walking. All he could do was complain.

"I don't wanta take over. I want you to find the son of a bitch, that's what I want. I want my share of the money, and I want to stop and rest for a while. That damn sun's gonna burn a hole in my hat."

"I told you we couldn't stop," Ben said.

He was getting tired of Jink's whining. He was also getting tired of Jink, period. They'd been partners for a good many years now, good times and bad, in prison and out, and they'd always stuck together, but Ben wasn't exactly the sentimental sort. It was beginning to look to him as if Jink couldn't hold up his end of the partnership anymore. Ben thought maybe it was time they split up.

He was sure of it about an hour later when Jink quietly slid out of his saddle and hit the ground. Jink was riding a little behind Ben, and if Jink's bay hadn't shied and whinnied when Jink fell, Ben might not have known about it until much later. They hadn't been doing much talking for the last few miles.

Ben caught up the reins of Jink's horse first and tied them to a bush before he checked on Jink.

Jink's face was red from more than the sun, and he was sweating heavily. The fever was on him again. He was muttering something under his breath, but it was just gibberish. Ben couldn't understand a word of it.

It was getting on toward late afternoon, and the sun was lowering in the west. There was enough of a breeze to cool things off, but Ben didn't think Jink could even feel the breeze. He grabbed his partner under the arms and dragged him to the shade of a small cedar and propped him up against the trunk. Jink was still mumbling incoherently. His eyes were shut tight.

Ben left him there and went back to Jink's horse for a canteen. He opened it, tilted Jink's head back, and poured a little water into his mouth.

Jink sputtered out the first swallow, but then he began to drink greedily. Ben had to take the canteen away before Jink drank all the water that was in it.

Jink sagged back against the tree, and Ben looked at his hand. The bandage that O'Grady had put on the finger was sweated and dirty, and the whole hand looked swollen to Ben. Even the arm was swollen and red.

"Ben?" Jink said, startling him. "You there, Ben?"

"I'm here," Ben said, wondering why Jink didn't open his eyes. "What the hell's the matter with you, Jink?"

"Don't know. Feel funny. Did we eat today?"

It was a peculiar time to be talking about food, Ben thought, but he said, "No. We didn't have time."

"We got anything?"

"Maybe some jerky," Ben said.

He didn't think it would be a good idea for Jink to

eat jerky, though. Too salty, and Jink didn't have that much water left in his canteen.

"Get me some, would you?" Jink said.

Oh, hell, Ben thought. *I might as well.*

He got a strip of jerky out of the saddlebags and handed it to Jink, who bit a piece off the end and started chewing it.

"Hell of a note, ain't it, Ben?" he said, continuing to chew as he spoke. His eyes were still closed, and he was talking very softly.

Ben squatted down so that he could hear. "What's that?" Ben said.

"Comin' to the end of the trail like this," Jink said. "A hell of a note." He took another bite of jerky, twisting the strip of dried meat with his teeth to tear off a piece.

"We ain't at the end," Ben said. "We still gotta catch that damn O'Grady and get our money from him."

"I don't think I'll be doin' any more chasin'," Jink said. "You want any of this jerky?"

"Nope," Ben said. "You finish it."

"Don't want no more of it." Jink let his hand fall to his lap, though he did not drop the jerky. "You're gonna leave me here, ain't you, Ben?"

That was exactly what Ben planned to do, all right. There was nothing he could do for Jink, except maybe throw him across his saddle and lead his horse along, and he wasn't about to do that.

"Yeah," Ben said. He didn't see any need to lie

about it. "I reckon I am. You don't look much like you can do any more chasin'. Like you said."

"Hell of a note," Jink said. "You gonna leave me my horse?"

Ben wanted to take the horse along, and if it'd been anybody else but Jink sitting there under that tree, Ben wouldn't have given it a second thought. But he'd been partnered with Jink too long. He wasn't sentimental, but he wasn't completely without feeling.

"Yeah," he said. "I'm gonna leave you your horse. He's tied right over there."

"I might get to feelin' better, is why I'm askin'," Jink said. He didn't open his eyes to look at the horse. "Might wanta catch up with you."

"Yeah," Ben said. "You probably will."

He didn't believe it for a second.

"Sure. You gonna leave me the canteen?"

"Yeah." *Why not?* Ben thought. *Wasn't hardly any water left in it.*

Jink didn't say anything for a while after that, and neither did Ben. Finally Ben said, "I gotta be goin', Jink. I can't let O'Grady get too far ahead of me."

"I know it," Jink said. "You go on. Just leave me my horse."

Ben stood up and looked down at Jink, who appeared to be three-quarters dead already. Jink didn't look up, didn't open his eyes.

Ben was walking toward his horse when he heard Jink call his name.

"What?" Ben said, turning back.

"If you catch up with that son of a bitch and get the money," Jink said, "you'll bring me my share, won't you?"

"Sure I will," Ben said. "You know me, Jink."

"Yeah, I know you, all right," Jink said, and Ben could have sworn there was a smile on his fevered face. "That's what's got me so worried."

They didn't bury Rawls Dawson after all.

"I don't think it would be a good idea," Jonathan said. "Somebody's bound to come out here lookin' for him sooner or later, and most likely sooner than later. If they don't find him, who knows what they'll think?"

"They won't find anybody else," Ellie pointed out. "We'll be gone."

She had accepted the fact that Jonathan was going with her. She wasn't sure why, but somehow the idea didn't seem objectionable.

"That's right," Jonathan said. "We won't be here, so we need to let whoever comes know what's goin' on."

They were back in the kitchen, drinking water again, and it tasted even better this time than before. Jonathan set his cup down on the table. "I think we better leave a note for 'em, let 'em know that I'm all right. We don't have to mention you."

Ellie wasn't too sure that she agreed. She didn't want anyone trailing along and interfering with her, but Jonathan eventually persuaded her that the note was the best idea. He found a pencil and a piece of paper in his office, and Ellie printed the note:

"Three men killed my son and the marshal. They are the ones who robbed the bank in town. I have gone to find them."

"Sounds about right," Jonathan said when he read it over. He took the pencil and signed his name on the paper.

"What do we do with it?" Ellie said.

"Pin it on the marshal."

They went outside, and Ellie took hold of Dawson's body and dragged it into the shade of the porch. She pulled him into a sitting position, his back against the wall, and then she pinned the note to his vest.

"Somebody better come looking before too long," she said, wiping the sweat from her forehead.

"I expect there'll be somebody before too long," Jonathan said. "When the marshal don't show up back in town, they'll be worried soon enough. We better get on our way. Can you ride a horse?"

"I have my wagon," Ellie said.

Jonathan sat on the porch, took off his hat, and fanned his face. He would have liked to ride in the wagon himself; in fact, he wasn't certain that he could ride a horse, though he was feeling surprisingly strong.

"I don't think that wagon can go where you'll want to be goin'," he said. "We won't be followin' any roads, and there's some mighty rough country around here, places where you'd break a wheel before you knew it. I don't reckon you're carryin' a spare."

"I can ride, then," Ellie said. "Do you have a horse?"

"Ought to be one or two in the barn. And we ought to put the marshal's horse in there."

They took care of the marshal's horse, and Ellie saddled two of Crossland's mares.

Jonathan went back into the house while she was occupied. He wanted to get his pistol.

He went into the kitchen then and took a few cans of sardines and tomatoes from the shelves. He carried them, along with the rifle, to the barn.

Ellie had the horses ready to go. She'd unhitched her mules and stabled them, and she'd slipped her shotgun into the rifle boot on one of the saddles.

Jonathan slid the Winchester into the boot on the other saddle and put the canned goods into the saddlebags.

"Ready?" he said.

"Yes," Ellie said, putting her foot into the stirrup and swinging into the saddle.

Jonathan didn't find mounting quite so easy. When he swung his leg over the saddle, he felt a wet pain slither through his midsection, and he bit down hard to keep from crying out. His face went white.

"Are you all right?" Ellie said.

Jonathan didn't answer for a while. He just sat in the saddle, trying to gain control of his breathing.

"Listen," Ellie said. "If—"

"I'm fine," Jonathan said before she could say anything more. "Let's go."

Ellie looked at him doubtfully. "You don't look fine to me," she said.

"Well, I am." Jonathan put his heels to the horse and guided it outside. "Are you comin', or not?"

"I'm coming." Ellie followed him out of the barn into the sunlight. "Do you know which way they went?"

"I think so. But that don't mean they kept goin' that way."

"Do you know anything about tracking?"

"Lord amighty," Jonathan said. "What were you goin' to do if I hadn't decided to come along? Try to smell 'em out?"

Ellie shook her head. "I really hadn't thought that far ahead. I guess I was just hoping they'd be at your ranch and I could settle with them here."

"Just settin' on the front porch, passin' the time and waitin' for you to shotgun 'em down," Jonathan said. "Is that what you thought?"

"I don't know what I thought. I just knew that I had to do something."

They rode in silence for a few minutes. Then Jonathan said, "I used to be able to track a cow over solid rock. Let one of them critters get away from the herd, I was the one that went after her. I could always find her and get her back. I reckon I can track three men on the run."

Ellie, who hadn't realized that she was holding herself quite so stiffly in the saddle, relaxed fractionally. She allowed herself a little bit of a smile.

"Good," she said.

Chapter 13

Jink didn't even know when Ben rode away. He slept fitfully most of the afternoon, his sleep troubled by crazy dreams so vivid that he was still horrified by them when he jerked awake. He didn't much want to remember them, but they had engraved themselves on his mind in such a way that they seemed even more real than the tree he was resting against or even the pain in his arm.

One of them had something to do with snakes, great diamondback rattlers that slithered up to him as he slept and crouched on his chest waiting for him to awaken so that they could strike him in the face. In the worst of those dreams, he was running from the place where he lay with five of the snakes, their fangs embedded in his cheeks and lips, hanging from his face.

In the other dreams, which were even worse, the Indian woman he and Ben killed up in Oklahoma came back to life and dug up her husband and both of them were chasing Jink across a landscape unlike anything he had ever seen before, a place of high hills made entirely of deep sand that Jink was forced to climb to escape and into which his feet sank deeper and deeper with every step he took, forcing him to use all his strength in freeing his feet from the shifting soil that was fighting to keep them in its grip.

The man and woman had no difficulty at all; they seemed to float above the sand, and their feet left no prints as they pursued Jink relentlessly. Their bodies were corrupted from having lain so long in the earth, and pieces of them kept falling off, little pieces, like a nose or an ear or a finger, and the pieces made a little trail to show the way they had come.

What with all the running through the sand in mortal terror from dead people or with snakes hanging from his face, Jink woke up more and more tired every time he dozed off, and a lot less eager to go back to sleep.

He was thirstier with every awakening, too. His mouth tasted as dry as if he had swallowed the sand instead of running in it.

He drank all his remaining water in one long gulp, shook the canteen, then threw it aside when he realized that it was empty. It clattered off a rock and lay still.

It was getting on toward late afternoon now. There was a little breeze from the west, and it was much cooler under the tree than it had been earlier, but Jink didn't know it. He was burning up.

He was wearing a dirty black vest over his shirt. The vest was unbuttoned, and he managed to slip it off. His shirt proved too much for him, however. He couldn't unbutton it, and he didn't have the strength to tear the buttons off, though he tried. He took off his bandanna and mopped his face and looked off into the distance.

There was nothing there to see, just a gray lizard that looked back at him for a few seconds before it slipped off the top of a rock and scuttled away.

"Ben?" Jink said, trying to sit up straighter. He failed and slumped back against the tree. "You out there anywhere, Ben?"

There was no answer except the neighing of Jink's horse, somewhere off to Jink's right. Jink turned his head, and the sight of the horse comforted him somehow. It was as if he hadn't been completely deserted. He mopped his face with the bandanna again, but the cloth was wet now and it didn't help much.

Jink dropped it onto his chest. His eyes closed slowly, and he drifted back into sleep.

O'Grady was doing fine until his horse threw him.

They were going down a little rocky hill when the noise of their progress disturbed a dozing rattler. The snake immediately coiled itself into a defensive posture and gave out its distinctive warning.

O'Grady's horse stopped short, planting its front feet and throwing O'Grady, who was too surprised to react, over its neck onto the hard ground.

O'Grady rolled over and over, scraping against the rocks, peeling skin off his hands, arms, and face. He brushed by a prickly pear with his left hand and filled the back of it with hundreds of tiny needles before he came to a stop at the bottom of the hill. A few small stones rolled down after him, and dirt filled his mouth and eyes.

The horse didn't stay around to watch. It reared up, rolled its eyes, turned and took off in the direction from which they'd come.

O'Grady sat up spitting and rubbed the dust out of his eyes with his right hand. He knew better than to get his left hand close to his eyes before he got the prickly pear needles out.

"Jesus, Mary, and Joseph," he said after he had spit most of the dirt from his mouth.

The snake shook its rattles again, and O'Grady looked back up the hill. The snake was coiled near a rock in the shade of a live oak not more than three feet tall. The snake's beady eyes were fixed on O'Grady, and its tongue flickered in and out of its mouth as it watched him steadily.

O'Grady unholstered his pistol, looked at it to see that its firing mechanism and barrel were clear of dirt, and without really thinking about it aimed at the rattler and pulled the trigger.

The pistol boomed and the head of the snake exploded. Its body uncoiled and whipped about in the dirt while the bullet tore on through the leaves of the oak and whanged off a rock higher up the hill.

"And that does for you, spawn of the devil that you are," O'Grady said.

He holstered the pistol and began painstakingly to pick the needles one by one out of the back of his left hand. It took a while, but he was patient and he got most of them. Then he got up to see if he could find his horse.

He told himself that he wouldn't have any trouble with the gelding. He couldn't afford to. The bag with the money was still tied to the saddle horn. He regretted having fired the shot, though. It might have spooked the horse, which was nervous anyhow on account of the snake.

O'Grady whistled low through his teeth. "Hey, boy," he called. "Hey, boy." He started walking slowly back up the hill.

It was only when he started walking that he noticed how much his right ankle was hurting him.

"Mother of Christ," he said, stopping to sit down again.

He pulled off his boot and peeled back a dirty, ragged sock to look at the ankle. It was swelling a bit, but as he felt it gingerly he told himself that it was not broken.

He pulled the boot back on and stood up again, then limped on up the hill whistling between his teeth. "Hey, boy," he said. "Hey, boy."

When he got to the top of the hill, he didn't see the damn horse anywhere.

Ben had just about given up on finding O'Grady when he heard the pistol shot.

After leaving Jink, Ben had followed O'Grady's trail as best he could, but he'd lost it again before too long. He thought about turning back and checking on Jink, but he couldn't see the profit in doing that. He thought he'd just ride until dark, maybe make camp, and then try following O'Grady again the next day.

Ben wasn't sure that O'Grady would stop for the night, but he was damn sure not going to try any tracking after dark. Hell, he couldn't even do it during the daylight.

He was looking around for a likely spot when he heard the gunshot. It was faint and a long way off, but there was no mistaking what it was, and although Ben's mind didn't work very fast, he was able to reason out that there really wasn't much likelihood of anyone except for O'Grady to be firing a gun in that deserted area.

The trouble was that sounds did funny things in the late afternoon air of the hill country. Ben couldn't be exactly sure just where the shot had come from.

He stood in his stirrups and looked around for a couple of minutes, but there were no clues to help him out, just the blue sky turning orangey red on the horizon and a few hazy purple clouds covering most of what was left of the sun.

He looked down for tracks, but there was no help on the ground, either. If there were tracks there, Ben sure as hell couldn't see them.

He closed his eyes and tried to concentrate, to remember precisely how the gunshot had sounded to him, hoping to get a clue from that as to its direction.

There was no help in doing that, either.

Then it occurred to Ben that if he was close enough to O'Grady to hear a gunshot, he must have been more or less on the right track all along. He'd been blundering along in the right direction, whether he knew it or not. So why not keep going in that same direction?

He nudged the horse ahead. He was sure looking forward to seeing O'Grady again.

As the two of them rode along, Jonathan told Ellie a little about his troubles with his son and how they had led up to the bank robbery.

"Gerald was never the kind of son I thought he should be," Jonathan said. "He was too soft, too lazy, and I let him know it. I guess that might have been a part of the trouble."

Ellie didn't know how to respond, not having any children of her own. She'd always thought that you'd just naturally love a child, no matter what it was like, so she said that.

"Maybe that's the way it ought to be," Jonathan said. "But it ain't. Least it wasn't with Gerald. I tried to love that boy, I surely did. But it just seemed like me and him was too different. If his ma, God rest her, had lived, things might have worked out better. Maybe she could've loved him enough for the both of us."

Ellie didn't see how that could be.

"You're probably right," Jonathan said. "I guess maybe I ought not to worry about it now. The boy's dead, and there's nothin' I can do to help him now. But I'll always look back and wonder what I could have done different. And I'll always wish I could've changed things for the better."

Ellie thought about her own life. There wasn't much she would want to change, except for all the events of the previous day. The rape would never have happened, and she and Burt would be together again.

"You can't do that, though," Jonathan said, interrupting her thoughts. "You can't change what's past by wishin'."

"No," Ellie said. "You can't do that."

"Might make life a mite easier if you could," Jonathan said, shifting in the saddle.

Ellie gave him a look.

"Don't you go wishin' you'd tried harder to talk me out of comin' along," Jonathan said. "You can't change that, either, and I ain't goin' back."

He was riding easier than he'd thought he would. The pain that had hit him in the barn had passed, and the only trouble he was having now was that he was weak from having spent too much time in bed. It had been too long since he'd ridden in a saddle. He knew that if he lived through the night, he'd be sore as hell in the morning.

"I don't wish you hadn't come along," Ellie said. "I don't think I'd have gotten this far without you."

She was being truthful. She could never have done any tracking, but thanks to Jonathan, they hadn't had nearly as much trouble following the men they were looking for as Ben and Jink had trying to follow O'Grady.

For one thing, Jonathan was nearly as good a tracker as he said he was, and his eyesight was remarkable for a man of his years. He could see signs on the ground that Ellie would have missed completely.

And for another thing, they were following three men, not just one. Three horses left a lot more sign than one did if you knew how to look for it, and Jonathan did.

He knew how to interpret what he saw, too. He would kick apart a horse apple and say, "Looks to be fresh. Not more than an hour old. We're gaining on 'em."

Ellie didn't doubt him for a second.

He figured out O'Grady's trick at the river quickly, but that was because Ben and Jink hadn't been trying to hide where they were going.

"Don't take no Injun to figger those two out," Jonathan said. "They're in a hurry, and they don't think there's anybody on their backtrail. Makes things easy."

"Maybe for you," Ellie told him.

"Yeah," Jonathan said. "Maybe."

He was standing by the edge of the water, holding his horse's reins, and looking across at the other side. "Here's where they went over. You can see the way the bank's chewed up on the other side there. They weren't tryin' to hide their tracks."

"Let's go, then," Ellie said. She was eager to get on with it.

"Tell you the truth, I could use me a little bit of a rest," Jonathan said. "Have a drink of this river water, maybe eat a can of those sardines I brought."

Ellie looked as if she might object, but she didn't.

"All right," she said. "But let's cross over first."

"I was thinkin' that there was a pretty good spot for a rest right here," Jonathan said, looking back and gesturing toward a clump of trees.

Ellie wondered if he really wanted a brief rest or if he were just unable to climb back into the saddle. Still, she didn't say it.

Instead she looked at the sky. "It's getting late. Do we have time to stop?"

"Got to stop sooner of later. Give the horses time to water. Get their breath back. Can't just keep goin' without a stop."

"What about when it gets dark?"

"We'll worry about that later. Oughta be another full moon tonight. You can see a lot with a moon like that if it don't come up a bunch of clouds."

Ellie vaguely remembered how the moon had

looked the night before when she rode to town, following the Stones in her wagon. She decided that Jonathan was right.

"Do you think those men will keep on riding?"

"Never can tell what a man like that'll do. If it was me, and if I thought there was maybe the chance of someone comin' after me, I'd ride as long as I could."

"But you said they didn't know we were back here," Ellie said.

"They don't, maybe. But the one leadin' the chase knows those other two are in back of him, or he ought to. Those fellas ain't the kind to let money get away from 'em. Now are we gonna rest a spell here or not?"

"Here's fine. What do you have besides sardines?" Ellie didn't like sardines. Too oily and salty for her.

"Tomatoes," Jonathan said.

Ellie thought about Jink and Ben.

"I think I'll just have a drink of water," she said.

Chapter 14

·──━═◆═━──·

It was late afternoon when Shag Tillman rode up to the Crossland ranch house. Tillman was a big, rawboned man, and he'd been the deputy marshal in Blanco for nearly five years. It was a job that suited Tillman, who didn't much favor the idea of hard work and responsibility. As Dawson's deputy, all he had to do was show up at the little jail and do what Dawson told him. He could handle that all right.

When Rawls Dawson had told Tillman that he'd be riding out to the Crossland place to talk to Gerald about the bank robbery, Shag had laughed about it.

"That jug-head don't have nerve enough to somethin' like rob a bank," he said, shaking his head.

"He might set that fire, though," Dawson said.

Shag thought about it. "He might at that. I expect he's a sneaky one, all right. You want me to ride out there with you?"

Dawson didn't think so. "I ought to be able to

handle somebody like Gerald Crossland," he said. "You stay here in case the Rangers come in. You can fill 'em in on what happened."

"Fine by me," Shag said.

But when Dawson rode away, Shag got to worrying about it. What if the robbers had gone to ground at Crosslands? It wasn't very likely, he had to admit, but it was possible. He hoped that Dawson knew what he was riding into.

Shag wasn't the type to worry too long about anything, however. He spent most of the day loafing around town, and he didn't think about Dawson again until the middle of the afternoon.

I wonder why he ain't come back, Shag thought. *Maybe I ought ride on out there.*

He didn't, however. It was a hot day, and he couldn't believe that Dawson could really be in trouble. Things like that just didn't happen around Blanco.

But the bank robbery had happened, and a little later on Shag saddled his horse and rode out to Crosslands.

He saw the marshal's body on the porch right away.

"Goddamn," he said, dismounting and stepping up on the porch beside it.

He unpinned the note and read it, running his finger along underneath the words and moving his lips as he did so.

"I'll be go to hell," he said when he'd finished. He looked down at Dawson's body. "I'll just be go to hell."

He knew he had to get Dawson back to town, but he didn't know what to do after that. Old Jonathan Crossland was already on the trail. Maybe that was good enough. Or maybe it wasn't. He wished that Dawson were alive to tell him what to do.

Then he thought about the Rangers. They would be in town soon, and they'd know what to do. He was pretty sure that it was too late to start after anybody now, and he had to get the marshal's body back to town let folks know what happened. That was his job.

Or at least he thought that was his job. He looked down at Dawson again.

"Damn," he said. "Why'd you have to go and get yourself killed and leave me all this worryin'?"

Dawson didn't say anything, not that Shag had expected him to.

"I guess I better see if I can find a horse to take you back to town on," Shag said. "I'll be right back."

He started toward the barn. He hoped the Rangers would be in town by the time he got back.

Ben was as quiet as he could be, which wasn't very quiet, and he knew it.

"Son of a bitch O'Grady could hear me comin' a mile off," Ben said to himself.

As he got closer to where he thought the shot must have come from, he decided to leave his horse and go along on foot. He wouldn't make quite as much noise that way.

He tied the reins to the limb of a scrawny oak and started off. The sun was just about down now, but there was still plenty of light in the sky to see by. Nevertheless Ben drew his pistol to have it ready in case he blundered onto O'Grady before he was ready for him.

That wasn't the way it happened, however. As it turned out, Ben saw O'Grady in plenty of time.

Ben was standing in the shadow of a tall cedar when O'Grady topped the hill he'd recently rolled down the other side of.

Ben wondered what the hell the Irishman was walking for, but he decided it didn't make any difference. It just made things easier for Ben, who lifted his pistol and sighted down the barrel at O'Grady.

His finger was tightening on the trigger when he heard a low whistle. Then he heard O'Grady call, "Here, boy. Where are you, boy?"

What the hell? Ben thought. Had the son of a bitch lost his horse? And then Ben thought about the bag of cash. O'Grady would have tied it to the saddle. He lowered his pistol.

O'Grady started down the hill, whistling and calling softly.

Ben smiled. The bastard had lost his horse, all right. This was going to be easier than Ben had thought. And a hell of a lot more fun, too.

———

When he had finished eating, Jonathan walked down to the river and washed out the sardine can before he put it back in the saddlebags. He'd seen too many cans rusting by the trail in his time, and besides that, he didn't believe in leaving any more signs of his passing than he could help. You never knew who might be coming along after you, looking to find you for one reason or another.

"You ready to get goin'?" he said.

Ellie hated to admit it, but she was pretty sure that she had needed the rest as much or more than Jonathan had. The day had been very hot, hotter than she'd expected, and she was not any more used to riding a horse than Jonathan was. She'd begun to suspect that he'd asked for the stop more for her benefit than for his own.

Her joints cracked when she stood up, and she could feel the pain in her thigh muscles.

"I'm ready when you are," she said, trying not to reveal how she felt.

Jonathan smiled as if she weren't hiding a thing.

"It ain't goin' to get much better," he said. "In fact, when you climb in that saddle, it's probably goin' to burn you like fire."

Ellie didn't ask how he knew. "I'll be fine," she told him, but she couldn't keep from sucking in her breath sharply as she rose in the stirrup.

Jonathan mounted up beside her. "You'll get used to it after a day or two or three."

"You don't think it will take that long?"

"Most likely."

Jonathan knew one thing for sure, though. He knew that he wasn't going to last that long. He was able to get into the saddle and stay there, and he felt sure he could ride all night. But somehow, he didn't think there was much more than that in him. If they had to go another day, even half a day, he wasn't going to be around to see the finish.

The thought saddened him, but not because he dreaded the idea of his own death. That was something he'd come to accept quite a while back, and there had even been a couple of particularly low times when he'd more or less wished for it.

But things were different now, he realized. He'd come to have a strong liking for Ellie Taine. She was the kind of woman he'd once hoped that Gerald would marry someday—strong, determined, and proud.

Of course a woman like that would never have looked twice at Gerald. As far as Jonathan knew, no other woman ever had either, not unless Gerald paid for her. Jonathan knew about his son's occasional trips to Mexico, and he had a pretty good idea why Gerald went there. There were whores aplenty a lot closer to Blanco than that, but Gerald was the kind who wouldn't want to risk his reputation so near to home.

It suddenly occurred to Jonathan that Mexico must have been where Gerald had met the bank robbers. They were the kind of men that Gerald would never have run across in Blanco, would never have associated with if he had. Gerald was too much of a

snob for that. But in another country, probably lik-
kered up, Gerald would have had the courage to ap-
proach them.

"Did you know my son?" Jonathan said.

"I saw him in town sometimes," Ellie said. "He
wasn't very friendly."

"No," Jonathan said. "I don't guess he was."

Jink didn't know what it was that woke him up, but he
knew it was something out of the ordinary. All the
other times, he'd jerked out of sleep as if someone had
hold of his shirt and was pulling him, but this time was
different.

He had a crick in his neck, and his back was hurting him because he'd been leaning against the tree for
so long. The damn thing was hard as hell, but that
wasn't what had wakened him.

It wasn't his finger, either, though the pain had
spread up nearly to his shoulder now, and his arm was
throbbing so hard with every heartbeat that Jink
thought he could see the skin bulging out and sinking
back in.

He'd almost gotten used to that, however. There
was a sort of regular rhythm to it that was almost
soothing if you thought about it in the right way.

Bump. Bulge. Sink. Bump. Bulge. Sink.

It was regular enough to put a man to sleep, but
Jink forced himself not to think about it, not to fall
into the easy, lulling rhythm of the beats.

He opened his eyes to look around for whatever it was that had disturbed him, but he didn't see anything unusual. It was a lot darker now than it had been the last time he'd waked up, but that was all.

He closed his eyes and tried to concentrate. He knew there was something wrong, but he just couldn't quite figure out what it was.

He thought for a minute that he might just be imagining things. He knew that he was in a bad way, and knew that a fever like the one he had could do funny things to a man's mind. Maybe that was all it was.

Then he heard voices, or thought he did. He strained his ears to hear what they were saying, but he couldn't. He could tell it was somebody talking, though. He was sure he wasn't imagining it.

That was what had made him wake up. There was someone talking close by.

He kept listening. He heard a horseshoe click against a rock, and he worked himself up until he was sitting a little straighter against the tree.

It wasn't easy. He had to push himself along with his good elbow and dig his boot heels into the dirt. It made his arm throb harder than ever. But he did it.

His blood was rushing in his ears, but he could still hear the talking. He knew it wasn't Ben and O'Grady. They wouldn't be talking friendly like the voices Jink could hear. So who the hell could it be?

He wondered if he could stand up. If he could, by

God, he'd find out who it was. He didn't think it would be anyone he wanted to see.

By pushing with his heels and scrunching his back along the trunk of the tree, he managed to stand. After that he didn't do anything for a while. His head felt about three times its normal size, and he was so weak and dizzy that he wasn't sure his legs would hold him up.

The dizziness passed finally, but then he noticed how much his arm was hurting. Well, that didn't matter. He knew what he was going to do.

He waited until his head was about as clear as it was going to get, and then he tottered off in the direction of the voices.

"They came by here somewhere," Jonathan said. He'd lost the trail a while back, but he was sure he and Ellie were headed in the right direction. "We'll pick 'em up before long."

"We'd better," Ellie said. "The sun's going down."

"Don't matter. I can follow 'em anyhow."

Ellie was beginning to have her doubts. Jonathan didn't seem quite as strong as he had earlier, and she was worried that they wouldn't be able to pick up the trail again, especially if it got dark.

She thought about what she would do if they didn't, and to her surprise she realized that she didn't really care any longer.

She wondered why, but not for long. She was normally a sensible woman, and she knew now that what she was doing was not sensible. In fact, she thought, she was acting just like Burt had, in a way. He'd gone out to punish the men who'd raped his wife, and he'd gotten himself killed.

Now she was going out to punish the men who'd killed him.

And for what?

Nothing that she could do to them would ever bring Burt back. Nothing that she could do would help Burt, not in the least.

But what about herself? Couldn't she punish them for what they'd done to her?

Not really, and she knew it.

There was no way to take back from them what they had taken from her in the floor of the wagon. Killing them certainly wouldn't do it.

Whatever she had lost, it was something that she would have to find in herself, and it came to her then that it was something that she had never really lost after all.

It was still there, in her determination, and it was there in her realization that she no longer had to do anything at all to get it back. She could go back to Blanco and pick up her life again and manage pretty well. Things would never be the same as they had with Burt, and she'd have to work the farm double hard, but she could do that.

She started to tell that to Jonathan, but as she started to speak, he said, "There's the trail, right up there. I can see where somebody broke off a tree limb. They went by here, all right. You comin', or not?"

His tone was eager and excited, and that was when Ellie knew that Jonathan, for some reason or other, needed to find those three men even more than she did. What he'd told her at the ranch explained his attitude to some extent, but not completely.

That didn't matter, however. She realized that she still wanted to go on as much as he did, really. No matter how hard she tried to convince herself differently, she knew she couldn't leave the job undone.

She no longer believed she had to kill the three men, but she knew they had to be punished. The law could do that, and that was just fine, that was the way it should be, but she and Jonathan were going to give the law all the help they could. Otherwise, they'd both have lost something, one way or the other.

And she wasn't going to let that happen.

"I'm coming," she said.

Chapter 15

There was a little ridge of ground between Jink and the voices, so he didn't think there was much chance of anybody seeing him, but he didn't take any chances. The setting sun caused the scrubby cedars and oaks to cast long shadows on the rocky terrain, and Jink used the shadows for cover as he stumbled from one tree to the next.

It was a short journey, but not an easy one. The shadows seemed to Jink to be moving, and then he noticed that the trees were moving, too, which didn't seem right to him. A tree ought to stay in one place. He missed one when he put out a hand to steady himself, but he grabbed a limb and caught himself before he fell.

When he got near to the crest of the rise, he lay down on his belly, holding back the moan that tried to escape him. He scooted along, every scoot sending pain thrilling through him, until he could see over the top of the ridge.

What he saw scared him so much that he almost cried out. His heart speeded up so much that he thought his arm was going to burst with the pain and spray his blood all over the ridge.

He jerked down his head and tried to calm himself, but his breath was rushing in and out so fast that he was sure they could hear him on the other side of the ridge.

"They." There were two of them, that was for certain, but he told himself that it couldn't have been the two he thought it was. It just wasn't possible, but then it wasn't possible for trees to move, either, and they were damn sure moving.

He looked at the trees again. They weren't moving now, but by God they had been. Hadn't they?

If they hadn't been, then maybe he hadn't really seen who he thought he had when he looked over the ridge top. He knew he'd have to look again, to be sure.

He didn't want to look. He was afraid that they'd still be there, and he didn't know what the hell he'd do then.

He had to look, though. If they were there, they'd find him sooner or later. He had to get the drop on them if they were really there.

So he looked, and there they were all right, just like they'd looked back in Oklahoma before he and Ben had killed them.

It was the dead Indian woman and her dead husband, come looking for him, just like in his dream, except that they weren't all rotted or anything.

They looked pretty much like normal people, and they were sitting there on their horses, looking at the ground, trying to pick up his trail.

He jerked his head down again. They hadn't seen him this time, either, and that was good. It meant that he had a chance. He could kill them before they spotted him. He sure as to God hoped they'd stay dead this time.

He turned over on his back, eased his pistol out of its holster and pulled the hammer back slowly so as not to make any sound. He discovered that it was just as well that he was taking it slow. Pulling back the hammer took just about all the strength he had.

When the pistol was cocked, he lay there waiting until he thought he could lift it and fire. The man and woman were talking again, but he still couldn't make out what they were saying.

Probably talkin' Injun talk, he thought. *Or dead people talk.*

He turned over and looked across the top of the ridge as the two of them began riding away.

Pulling the trigger of the pistol was one of the hardest things he'd ever done. It came back slowly, slowly.

Finally, after what seemed to Jink like an hour, the pistol roared, and its powerful kick thrust it backward and out of Jink's nerveless hand.

———

O'Grady had been so close to what he was looking for out of life that he could taste it, but now he could feel it all slipping away from him.

It had seemed easy when he'd talked about it to Gerald Crossland down in Mexico. A small-town bank, not much law to speak of, and a lot of money in the bank, all for the taking. What could be easier? He'd just do that one little thing and then be well enough off never to have to resort to any kind of crime again.

But the money hadn't been there. That was galling enough, but then Ben and Jink had to get trigger-happy.

Well, things could still have worked out. There was as much money in the bag as he would have gotten as his share if things had gone well. He could do fine as long as he could keep it away from Ben and Jink, who, he was now convinced, were crazy as bedbugs.

And as long as he could keep clear of the law long enough to get to Mexico.

He didn't think the law would be a problem. He didn't really think he'd have any trouble eluding Ben and Jink, either, if he could just put enough distance between himself and them. They weren't likely to be smart enough ever to find him after a little time had passed, and he'd been on the very verge of getting away from them. He was sure of it, and if it hadn't been for that damn rattler, he'd be so far ahead of them that they'd never have seen him again.

Now, though, they were going to have a chance to catch up with him if he didn't find that horse soon.

Not only that, he didn't have the money. The damn horse did, and because of the damage to his ankle, he could hardly walk. He was sure now that he was never going to escape the kind of life he had been living. He was going to spend the rest of his life hiding from the law and trying to scrape together enough money to keep himself fed.

Maybe he shouldn't have shot the damn snake; maybe he should just have walked over and let it bite him. At least he'd have been out of his misery.

He didn't see how things could get much worse.

The sun was just about to sink below the horizon now, and there was a breeze that rustled in the leaves of the oaks. O'Grady hoped he could find the horse before dark.

He heard a rock click against something off to his right and turned in that direction. "Is that you, boy?" he said. "Come here now."

Ben, who had thrown the rock, stepped out of the shadows to the other side of O'Grady, his pistol pointed straight at the Irishman. "Ain't no boys over there," he said.

O'Grady whirled around, clawing at his own pistol as he turned. His ankle gave way under him with the sudden movement, and he fell sprawling to the side.

His pistol fell just out of his reach, and as he twisted himself to make a grab for it, Ben fired a shot into the dirt near his hand.

"Don't try that again," Ben said. "I'd hate to have to kill you before we had us a little talk."

O'Grady sighed. It never did to think things couldn't get any worse; as long as you were alive to think they couldn't, they damn sure could.

"All right if I sit up?" he said.

"Just don't do it too fast," Ben said. He walked over and picked up the fallen pistol and stuck it in his belt, never taking his eyes off O'Grady.

"Where's your horse?" he said when O'Grady was sitting up.

"That's just what I'm wanting to know, myself. You haven't seen him, by any chance?"

"Nope. You don't look any too light on your feet, either. What happened to you?"

"Rattler. Spooked the horse." O'Grady looked around. "And where might your partner be?"

"Jink? He took to feelin' poorly. Had to leave him back up the trail a ways."

O'Grady nodded. "I thought the blood poisoning might get to him. Still, a man ought not to go off and leave his partner."

"His idea, not mine," Ben said. "He was mighty sick."

It might even be the truth, O'Grady thought. "Sorry to hear it," he said.

"Yeah, I bet you are," Ben said. "Now why don't you tell me where my money is."

"Your money?" O'Grady shifted his position slightly. It was getting darker, the shadows getting deeper, but the full moon was already rising in the sky. Before long it would be giving plenty of light. O'Grady wasn't going to be able to get the jump on Ben unless something happened to distract him.

"Damn right, *my* money," Ben said. "Jink won't be needin' a share." Ben looked straight at O'Grady. "Nobody else will, either."

"What about that marshal?" O'Grady said. "He might think it ought to go back to the bank."

Ben just laughed, and O'Grady was sure the marshal was dead, just like he'd figured.

"I'm not worried about any marshal," Ben said. "Now, why don't you just tell me about the money so I can be gettin' on the trail. I'd like to get a little ways on down the road before mornin'."

O'Grady smiled. "I don't know where the money is."

"That's a damn lie," Ben said. "I don't want to have to kill you, O'Grady, but I'd just as soon do it right now if you don't tell me where the money is. I can find it without your help if I have to."

O'Grady knew that Ben was going to kill him anyway as soon as he had his hands on the money, but that didn't change the fact that O'Grady was telling the truth.

"I told you that I don't know where it is," he said. "That's the truth. It's still in that bag, tied to my saddle horn. And the saddle's on my horse."

"Well, ain't that a shame," Ben said. "I guess I'll

just have to find that horse and take that bag for my-self."

"That won't be easy," O'Grady said. "That horse and I have been through a lot together, and he won't be coming to anybody but me."

O'Grady didn't know whether that was true or not. But it might be. So far, he hadn't even been able to make the horse come to him.

"We got to find that horse before he goes roamin' too far off," Ben said. "Get your ass up." He lifted the barrel of the pistol to indicate that O'Grady should stand.

"I have a bad ankle," O'Grady said. "I'm not sure I can do any walking."

"You can walk, by God," Ben said. "You'll walk or you'll crawl, but either way we're gonna find that damn horse. Now get up."

O'Grady got up. His ankle didn't really hurt too much if he didn't put his full weight on it, but Ben didn't need to know that.

"I might be able to make it if you'd let me lean on you," he said.

"I ain't that dumb," Ben said. "You keep away from me and start lookin' for that horse. I'll be right with you."

O'Grady looked at the pistol that Ben had stuck in his belt, but Ben said, "You can forget that idea, old son. You won't be gettin' your hands on your pistol again."

O'Grady grinned. "You should be more trusting of your fellow man, Ben."

Ben snorted. "Hell with that. You just find that horse."

O'Grady started to walk with an exaggerated limp. "I'll try," he said.

"You better try damn hard," Ben said.

Jink's shot didn't hit anything, unless it was a tree off in the distance. The bullet whistled between Ellie and Jonathan and buzzed away.

Jonathan didn't waste any words. "Somebody's shootin'. Head for those trees." He took off at a lope, with Ellie close behind.

When they reached the shelter of the trees, Jonathan reined in, and Ellie did the same. The horses snorted and stamped.

Jonathan was turned in the saddle, trying to see where the shot had come from.

"Who could be shooting at us?" Ellie said.

"Couldn't be anybody else but those fellas we're after," Jonathan said. He thought the shot had come from the little ridge that he could see not too far away, but there was no sign of anyone up there now.

"Hidin' down on the other side," Jonathan said, half to himself.

"Who?" Ellie said. "Where?"

"Somebody's back of that ridge," Jonathan said, pointing and wondering why there had been no more shots. "Maybe they were just tryin' to scare us." He didn't really believe that, not for a minute.

"What should we do?" Ellie said.

Jonathan turned away from the ridge and looked at her. "Now that's a pretty good question. What do you think?"

"Me?" Ellie didn't understand.

"This here was mostly your idea," Jonathan said. "I was just comin' along for the ride."

"They killed your son," Ellie said.

"They did. And I'm sorry for it. But he was mixed up in somethin' that he should never've been a part of, and it got him killed. He was old enough to know better."

Ellie thought that was a hard attitude, and she said so.

"Maybe. I'm not sayin' that Gerald deserved what he got. I'm just sayin' he'd still be alive if he hadn't fooled around with robbers and killers. I came along with you because I needed to come, but what we do now is up to you."

"All right, then," Ellie said. She didn't want to talk about Gerald anymore. "What choices do we have?"

"Well, we could just try ridin' away. They might even let us. 'Course they might come after us, too. Or we can try goin' to ground somewhere. These trees won't hold 'em off for very long if they're serious about hurtin' us."

Ellie looked around her at the skinny oak trees,

most of them hardly any taller than her head as she sat on the horse. They didn't offer much shelter at all.

"Or we could go after 'em," Jonathan said. "That's what you came for, ain't it?"

Ellie remembered what she had been thinking only a short while before. "I guess it is," she said.

"Well, then," Jonathan said.

"All right," Ellie said. "We'll go after them. Will you tell me how?"

Jonathan smiled. "I guess I could do that," he said.

Chapter 16

━━◆━━

The moon was up over the tops of the trees, round and yellow, so bright that the evening stars were not yet visible, though it was dark in the trees and hollows where O'Grady and Ben were looking for the strayed horse, and night birds called in the distance.

"You ought not to ever have shot at that snake," Ben said. "What with that horse bein' spooked already, firin' a gun was enough to scare him to Mexico. Besides that, I'd never've found you if I hadn't heard the shot."

O'Grady was limping badly, trying to give the impression that he was suffering terribly from the pain in his ankle, and he put a bit of strain in his voice as he answered.

"I'm glad you're giving me that bit of advice," he said. "Sure and it's a world of good it's doing me now."

"Nothin's goin' to do you any good now," Ben said. He was tired of looking for the horse, which he figured was long gone. "We ain't never goin' to find that horse, so I might as well kill you and have done with it."

"Killing me won't do you any good," O'Grady said. "Why don't we make camp. We can stay here for the night, and then we can look for the horse again in the morning. He can't have gone far, and by tomorrow he'll be looking for me. There's not a lot of grass around here; he'll be wanting something to eat."

Ben thought about it. Maybe O'Grady had a point. But Ben didn't think there was any need for the Irishman to be doing any waiting.

He thumbed back the hammer of his pistol.

O'Grady heard the click. "Before you do something that you'll be regretting," he said, "let me remind you that the horse won't come to you. If he does come back, it's me that he'll be looking for."

Well, maybe so. Ben lowered the hammer.

"Where do you think we should be camping?" O'Grady said.

"Don't go tryin' to get friendly," Ben said. "This ain't gonna be no campfire party. I'll be keepin' an eye on you all night."

"And that will be fine with me. But where will we be staying?"

"We'll go back where I tied up my horse," Ben said. "That's as good a place as any."

It was what O'Grady had been hoping to hear. Having at the moment no horse of his own, he thought that his best bet was to get his hands on Ben's.

There were a number of obstacles that had to be overcome first, not the least of which was Ben's regrettable lack of trust, but that could be dealt with later. At least for now, it appeared that O'Grady would survive the night.

"A fine idea," he said. "And where might your horse be?"

"Back that way," Ben said, pointing to the right. "You go along in front."

"Of course," O'Grady said. He didn't mind. He wasn't going to try jumping Ben now. If he had to kill him, he might not be able to find the horse on his own, and then he would be no better off than he was now. He limped along in the direction that Ben had indicated, waiting for his chance.

Jink was panting as if he'd run up one of the sandy hills he had dreamed about. He scrabbled around in the dirt for his pistol and tried to keep from screaming from the pain that had now stretched from his hand all the way to his shoulder.

He knew he hadn't hit anyone with the shot he'd fired. By the time he'd pulled the trigger, his hand had been shaking so much that he couldn't have hit anything smaller than a house except by accident.

Which meant that the man and woman were both still out there somewhere.

And worse than that, it meant that they knew where he was hiding.

He had to get away from there.

He sobbed with relief as the fingers of his right hand closed around the checkered wooden grips of his pistol, and he pulled it to his chest and held it there for a moment while he tried to decide which way to go.

The ridge ran a little farther to his left than to his right, and at the left end there was a little more cover—some spindly cedars whose limbs grew almost down to the ground. It was getting dark now, and if he could get to the cedars, he might be able to hide there.

The cedars had a strong smell, too, which would be a big help. His left hand was smelling rank even to him, and he knew the dead people would be able to track him just by the smell if the cedars didn't mask it.

Still sobbing, he slid toward the bottom of the ridge, then rose to a half crouch and wobbled toward the trees, looking back over his shoulder every two or three steps to make sure that no one was following him.

No one was, but he nevertheless fell down twice, hard, on his way to the trees, tearing his pants and scraping the skin off both knees. He was barely able to keep from screaming the second time because he landed on his left arm.

When he got to the trees, he pitched forward and slid beneath the dark shelter of their branches. Sweat and tears were running down his face and into his mouth, and he swiped them away with the back of the dirty hand that held the revolver.

The limbs of the tree he was under nearly touched the ground, and they were so thick it was hard for him to sit up, but he managed it. The smell of the cedar tickled his nose, but he somehow kept himself from sneezing. The touch of the limbs made him itch, too, but anything was better than being out in the open.

It was very dark under the tree, and it was quiet except for Jink's sobbing and the clicking of some kind of insect.

Jink sat there shaking and trying to stifle the sound of his sobs. After a while, he calmed a bit, though his gun hand was still not entirely steady. He listened for his pursuers, but he heard nothing.

Maybe it was just another damn dream, he thought. But he knew that couldn't be so. He was hurting too much for it to be a dream. In fact, that had been the only benefit of sleeping. While he was dreaming, he wasn't in pain.

He looked down at his hand. It was hard to see it in the darkness, but he could tell that it was about twice its normal size and that the bandage was ragged and torn. It was probably filthy, too, but Jink didn't care about that. All he cared about was the dead people who were after him.

He had to take care of them first. Then he could worry about his hand.

Jonathan didn't know who had fired the shot from behind the ridge, but he had two ideas. It was either the one man who had ridden away before Rawls Dawson was shot, or it was the two who had killed Gerald and the marshal.

It was even possible that the three men had gotten back together, but Jonathan didn't think that had happened.

It seemed more likely that it was the one man alone, since there hadn't been any shots after the first one. Two men setting up an ambush would most likely have stationed themselves at opposite ends of the ridge and caught Jonathan and Ellie in a crossfire, but that wasn't the way it had happened.

In fact, there'd been only one shot, which puzzled Jonathan slightly. He couldn't figure out why the drygulcher hadn't kept right on firing, unless he'd just wanted a little extra time to get away rather than kill anyone.

Jonathan supposed that was possible, but knowing the kind of men they were dealing with, it didn't seem very likely. So he was going on the supposition that the man was still there, somewhere.

"We might sneak up on him," he said to Ellie. "If you're willin' to try it."

Ellie wasn't sure what she wanted to do. If he'd asked her an hour before, she wouldn't have hesitated, but now her feelings were all in a jumble.

She was no longer sure at all that she was interested in getting revenge, and she wasn't sure how she'd feel about it if she did. It had seemed to her that Jonathan was more interested in locating the three men than she was, but now when it appeared that they had caught up to them, Jonathan was leaving everything to her.

She had thought that she had things figured out, but somewhere along the way everything had changed. And she didn't know just exactly what the changes meant, or even what they were. The only thing she was sure of was that the object of the trip now wasn't the same as when she'd started out.

However, she still wanted the men to be punished. There wasn't any question about that. And if the law wasn't there to take them in, then maybe it was up to her.

"What do we do if we can sneak up on him?" she said.

"That's kinda up to him. I don't think we can count on him throwin' down his pistol and surrenderin' to us, though. Do you?"

Ellie thought about Burt, and about the bodies of Gerald Crossland and the marshal.

"No," she said. "I don't think he'd do that."

"Another thing," Jonathan said. "There might be two of 'em. Maybe even three."

"That makes it harder, doesn't it?"

"Maybe. You still want to try?"

"You didn't tell me what we had to do."

"If he shoots at us," Jonathan said, "we shoot back."

Ellie had to think about that for a while, though it was more or less what she'd expected. Earlier, it had been what she wanted. She still couldn't figure out what Jonathan wanted.

"All right," she said finally.

"You're sure about that?" Jonathan said. "You ever shot a gun at anybody before?"

"No. But I can do it."

Jonathan thought she was telling the truth. Considering what the men had done to her, he would have been surprised if she'd answered any other way.

"Here's what we'll do then," he said.

Shag Tillman made it back to Blanco about sundown, leading the marshal's horse, with the marshal lying across the animal's back, wrapped up in a horse blanket that Shag had taken from Jonathan Crossland's barn.

Several people saw him come into town, and they had a strong feeling they knew who was under the blanket. They followed Shag to Fowler's undertaking establishment and helped him take the marshal down and carry him inside.

One of the men was Elmer Wiley, the bank president. "What happened?" he said.

The men were outside again. Fowler had taken charge of things and gotten Rawls Dawson into the back room to prepare him for burial.

Shag showed Wiley the note that had been pinned to Dawson's vest.

"That crazy old fool," Wiley said. "He's three-quarters dead himself. What good does he expect to do?"

"I don't know about that," Shag said. "All I know's what that note says. He was a mighty good man in his day, so I've heard."

"And what do you plan to do?" Wiley said. "With Dawson dead, you're the law in Blanco."

Shag might be the law, but he didn't feel too self-important right at the moment.

"Those Rangers the marshal sent for get here yet?" he said.

"No one's seen them if they did," Wiley told him.

"I expect we'd better wait for them, then," Shag said. "We can't do anything tonight, anyhow, and they oughta be here by tomorrow for sure."

Wiley didn't argue. Dawson had been next to worthless, and now he'd gotten himself killed. And Shag Tillman made Rawls Dawson look like Wyatt Earp. Jonathan Crossland might have been a hell of a man in his day, but his day had been over for too many years for the past to count for anything now.

"Very well," Wiley said. "We'll wait on the Rangers."

He'd just about given up any hope of getting the bank's money back. By the time the Rangers arrived in Blanco, the robbers would be in Mexico.

They were coming for him.

Jink couldn't have said how he knew that, but he

knew. It was as if someone were whispering it to him in the slowly stirring branches of the cedar where he was concealed.

Well, let 'em come. He was ready for them. He'd killed them once, by God, and he could do it again. He'd had Ben's help the first time, but he could handle the job by himself if he could just quit shaking.

He didn't know what they wanted with him, anyhow. Why hadn't they gone after Ben? It seemed to Jink that killing them had been Ben's idea in the first place. Hadn't it? He couldn't remember. Maybe it hadn't been anybody's idea. Maybe it was just something they'd done. Hell, it wasn't his fault, either way. Wasn't no call for 'em to come ha'ntin' him out of their graves.

He heard a rustling in the cedars nearby. Here they came.

He steadied his hand on a branch as best he could, and waited.

Chapter 17

━━✦✦✦━━

Because he was in the lead, O'Grady saw the two horses before Ben did.

He was surprised that he hadn't thought of the two horses getting together. It was logical that if there was another horse in the vicinity, his own horse might somehow sense it and, being naturally sociable as some horses were, find his way to where the other horse was standing.

By the time O'Grady had reasoned it out, it was almost too late. Ben had seen the horses, too.

O'Grady was just a little bit quicker, however, both mentally and physically, so that by the time Ben had jerked out his pistol and started triggering it, O'Grady had jumped to the side, rolled over, and come up running.

"You son of a bitch," Ben roared, firing his revolver until the hammer clicked over an empty cylinder.

O'Grady heard bullets whizzing over his head, and one of them nicked a small cedar branch that fell in his face, but that was as close as Ben came to hitting him.

His ankle felt as if it had been kicked by a horse, and his leg almost went out from under him a couple of times, but he kept running, weaving in and out among the few trees that were there to offer him cover, trying not to get too far away from the horses.

He knew that Ben would figure out soon enough that killing him, while it might offer a certain amount of personal satisfaction, didn't matter nearly as much as getting his hands on the money did.

O'Grady didn't want to die, and he didn't want Ben to have the money, either. So he planned to get to it first. There was a loaded rifle in the boot fastened to his saddle girth. If he could get to it and get it out before Ben shot him, he had a chance.

Fortunately, his horse had calmed down since the encounter with the rattler, and the presence of another horse also helped soothe him. At any rate, neither of the mounts was spooked by Ben's shots.

O'Grady angled back to his left not running now but moving quietly, keeping as best he could to the sparse cover, trying to move among the shadows and keep out of Ben's line of sight.

Something of what O'Grady had in mind must have occurred to Ben, who suddenly started running toward the horses. He raised his pistol, trying to reload on the run, but his fingers were clumsy, and he dropped it.

He didn't stop to pick it up. Instead, he pulled O'Grady's gun from his belt and held it carelessly as he ran.

O'Grady heard him coming and gave up all pretense at caution. He broke into a faltering run, nearly going down each time his ankle took his weight, but managing to stay upright. He was almost there.

Ben saw him coming and came to a sudden stop. He raised the pistol and fired.

As Ben discovered, running and shooting do not go well together. The brisk activity did nothing for the steadiness of his aim, and the bullet didn't even come close to O'Grady.

Ben forced himself to take a deep breath and to squeeze the trigger slowly. His second shot ripped through O'Grady's shirt near the ribs on the right side, grazing O'Grady's ribs.

O'Grady threw himself forward and skidded toward the horses on his belly, the rough ground tearing his shirt and the rocks ripping his skin. He slid under his horse and grabbed the stirrup to pull himself up.

He stayed half bent so that his head wouldn't show over the saddle, but Ben kept shooting. He was shooting at O'Grady's legs.

O'Grady tugged the rifle from the boot. He waited until he had control of his breathing. Then he stood up and brought the rifle over the top of the saddle.

There was still enough light in the sky for him to see Ben.

Ben realized what was going to happen, but it was too late for him to do anything about it. O'Grady pulled the trigger, and the bullet slammed into Ben's right shoulder, turning him sideways and causing him to lose his balance. He fell to the ground, the pistol dropping from his hand.

O'Grady walked out from behind the horse, keeping the rifle aimed at Ben. He saw that he didn't have anything to worry about. Ben was sitting on the ground, his teeth clenched, his left hand clutching his bleeding shoulder.

"Well, Ben," O'Grady said. "Not feeling too likely a lad, now, are you?"

"You turd," Ben said.

"Ah, Ben, that's no way to talk to a friend. If you'd only been a wee bit more trusting of me, it would never have come to this."

"The hell it wouldn't. You'd have gone for me as soon as you got to that rifle, whether I'd trusted you or not."

"Well, we'll never know that, will we? The question is, what do we do now?"

Ben just scowled at him.

"Oh, I'd know what *you'd* do," O'Grady said. "You're not the kind even to give it much thought. You'd be shooting me where I sat if we exchanged places. But I'm a bit more on the thoughtful side, myself."

"The hell you are. Why don't you quit your yappin'. Just shoot me and get it over with?"

O'Grady lowered the rifle until the barrel was pointing at the ground.

"I don't think I will," he said. "I don't think I need to, not now."

Ben couldn't figure it. "What're you gonna do, then?"

"What you did to Jink?"

"You're just gonna leave me here? Jesus, you can't do that, O'Grady." He looked at his shoulder, where the blood was seeping between his fingers. "I'm bleedin' to death. If you leave me here, I'm gonna die."

"And what did you think was going to happen to Jink?"

"That's different."

"I'm afraid I don't see it that way," O'Grady said.

"Well, it is. Jink and me was partners. He knew he was gonna die, and he didn't want to slow me down."

"I don't want you slowing *me* down, either. So I'll be leaving you now."

He bent down and retrieved his pistol. After he returned it to his holster, he went back to his horse and slid the rifle into the boot.

He patted the bag of money. "It's all in here," he called to Ben. "I don't think you'll be needing your share, any more than Jink will."

"You gonna leave me my horse?" Ben said.

"Well, now, that's something to be thinking

about," O'Grady said. He looked at Ben's horse speculatively.

"I left Jink's horse for him."

"That was fine of you, wasn't it? But maybe I'm not quite as big a man as you are, after all."

O'Grady mounted his own horse and reached over to untie Ben's reins from the tree branch. He nudged his horse forward with his knees and led Ben's horse away.

"You son of a bitch," Ben yelled after him.

O'Grady smiled, but he didn't look back.

Jonathan's plan was simple. He would go around the ridge in one direction, while Ellie would go the other way. They would catch the gunman in the middle.

If the gunman hadn't already moved out.

Jonathan didn't think that had happened. He hadn't heard a horse, though a man could have gotten away on foot to a horse that had been hidden elsewhere.

He just hoped that the man hadn't gone around the end where Ellie was headed.

He peered into the cedars in front of him. They surrounded the far end of the ridge, and he'd first thought about sending Ellie that way because of the cover they would provide for her. But then he'd thought better of it. If someone were waiting on them, that's where he'd be waiting. Jonathan thought it would be better if he went that way.

He wouldn't mind meeting up with one of those fellas in the least.

He had his pistol drawn, and when he heard a noise in the cedars, he lifted it and pointed it in the general direction of the sound.

The trees were dark, but he saw the branches rustling in one of them. Then he saw the moonlight glint off metal, and he fired at the glint.

The bullet slashed through the cedar branches well above Jink's head, missing him by a good three feet. Under ordinary circumstances, such a miss wouldn't have caused Jink to turn a hair, but Jink was not ordinarily half delirious.

Almost as soon as the shot was fired, Jink came thrashing out of the tree, waving his arms to clear the way.

Jonathan didn't recognize him, but he knew he wasn't a friend. He snapped off another shot at him, missing again by a wide margin. Then he followed Jink.

Jink was yelling something about dead people and running away like a cringing animal, flinging looks at Jonathan over his shoulder.

Ellie rounded the bottom of the ridge at the opposite end. She was holding the shotgun as if she meant to use it as soon as Jink got close enough.

Jink stopped looking back just in time to get a glimpse of Ellie as she raised the shotgun. He screamed even louder and stopped dead, his head swiveling from Ellie to Jonathan and back again.

Strings of saliva hung from his lips and whipped around his face as he jerked his head back and forth. In the moonlight, the two people at the ends of the ridge looked more dead than ever, the pale light silvering their faces and the slight breeze rippling their clothing like ghostly vestments.

Ellie knew who the man was, though she couldn't see his face. His size was enough. She was not frightened of him, however, and she didn't want to kill him. Her strongest emotion was pity.

Nevertheless, she did not lower the shotgun, though she was not sure she would be able to pull the trigger, not even if the man got closer.

"Over here," Jonathan called. "You come on thisaway, fella."

He stood there waiting. He had lowered his pistol again and seemed relaxed, as if he were waiting for something far different from a man with a gun.

Jink looked at him, and then he looked at Ellie, who was still holding the shotgun ready.

Jonathan must have looked like the better bet, and Jink turned back toward him. He staggered two steps in that direction; then he raised his pistol, steadied it as best he could, and fired.

The bullet plowed up the dirt at Jonathan's feet. Jonathan didn't even move. He just stood there, still waiting.

Jink's hand was shaking as if he were palsied, but he managed to get off another shot.

It chinged off a rock near Jonathan's right boot, but the old man still didn't move.

Ellie watched all this with puzzlement at first, and then with growing horror. She started running toward Jink. She knew that she had to shoot him now, no matter what she had thought at first. Otherwise, he was going to kill Jonathan. The fact that Jonathan seemed to want to die didn't mean she shouldn't try to prevent it.

"Stop it!" she said. "Stop it!"

Jink whirled to face her. He was clearly terrified, his eyes and mouth wide with fear.

"Go away!" he yelled. "You're dead! You're dead!"

He was trying to aim his pistol as he yelled. Jonathan was afraid to shoot him, afraid that he might hit Ellie. His aim was by no means as certain as it had once been.

He tried yelling to distract Jink, but Jink's attention was now riveted on Ellie.

"Shoot him, Ellie," Jonathan said, hoping that she would do it before it was too late. "Do it now."

Ellie heard him, and her finger tightened on the trigger. She didn't think that she would be able to do it, but the thought of how Burt looked in the coffin flashed into her head, and she remembered exactly how hard her head had hit the bed of the wagon when Jink had struck her. She remembered with sudden clarity the sound that it had made.

The hammers of the shotgun were already cocked. She pulled the trigger.

Chapter 18

O'Grady was a happy man. He was free of Ben and Jink, he had his bag of money, and there was no one on his trail. The moon was a golden yellow in a clear black sky, and if there were no further interruptions of his journey, he would be in Mexico before he knew it.

His ankle was hurting him, true, but he was sure that it was only twisted, not broken; he'd get over that soon enough. His shirt was ripped, and the places where the bullet and rocks had scraped off his skin were stinging a bit from the sweat of his recent exertions, but the night was cooling rapidly and the sweat was drying. There was no real pain, and what there was hardly bothered him at all.

He was a little sorry about leaving Ben like that. They'd been what passed for friends when they'd been in prison. But the truth of the matter was that Ben would have killed him in a minute. Hell, he'd *tried* to kill him. Whatever happened to Ben, Ben deserved it.

It was too bad about Jink, too, but Jink was bound to die from the blood poisoning. From the way he'd looked that morning, O'Grady would be surprised if he were still alive. Maybe a doctor could have done something for him, but there weren't any doctors out there in the scrub country, and even if there had been, it would be too late now. Going back to look for Jink never entered O'Grady's mind.

O'Grady clucked to his horse to urge it forward and began to whistle a little jig. Life was good again.

Ben was not suffering badly. Just as O'Grady had exaggerated his problems with his ankle to fool Ben, Ben had exaggerated the pain of his wound to mislead O'Grady.

The bullet had passed through the meaty part of Ben's shoulder, and it was causing him a certain amount of suffering, but he was not completely impaired.

It took him a while, but he managed to tear apart his shirt and rig a bandage of sorts, not a very clean one, but better than nothing. He was able to get it tied tight enough to stop the bleeding. O'Grady had left him his pistol, so he wasn't going to be unprotected.

The question was, what was he going to do? Go back to where he had left Jink, or go after O'Grady?

Ben wasn't very good at thinking things through, but it occurred to him that he would never have a chance if he went after O'Grady on foot. He would never catch up with him.

And he sure as hell couldn't do Jink any good. On the other hand, there was some good that Jink might do for Ben. Jink had a horse that he wouldn't be needing anymore. In fact, by the time Ben got back to where the horse was waiting, Jink would almost certainly be dead.

Ben started walking back in the direction he'd come from earlier. He didn't have any idea how long it would take him to get to Jink on foot, especially at night, but it didn't make any difference. He had to get there. Getting to that horse was the only chance he'd have to catch O'Grady.

O'Grady was going to have quite a head start, but the Irishman would be cocky, never dreaming that Ben was still after him. Sooner or later Ben would catch up with him. And then he'd kill O'Grady and get the money.

Thinking about it made Ben feel a little better. Walking wasn't going to help his wound much, but he couldn't just sit where he was. He'd need to eat sooner or later, and he needed water now. That son of a bitch O'Grady had taken his canteen along with his horse.

Well, he'd left some water with Jink, if Jink hadn't drunk it all. Maybe he'd died before he could drink it. Ben sort of hoped so.

———

When the shotgun roared, Jink's mind suddenly cleared.

He knew with a terrible certainty that the woman he was looking at was not the Indian woman from Oklahoma after all.

It was that other woman, the one from the wagon only the day before.

He wanted to tell her that he knew her and to beg her not to shoot him, but of course he didn't have the time.

He wanted to tell her that it hadn't been his idea. He'd never have touched her if it hadn't been for his partner. He didn't have the time to tell her that, either.

And he wanted to tell her that she didn't need to kill him. She'd already done that when she got her spit in the cut on his finger, sure as if she'd shot him in the gut. He was as good as dead already; shooting him was just going to get rid of him a little bit faster.

All those things went through Jink's mind in the fraction of an instant between the crash of the gun and the time the buckshot ripped right on through him, blasting apart the right side of his chest and leaving his right arm attached to the shoulder by nothing more than a sinew.

He took a sort of hopping step backward and fell heavily on his ruined side.

He lay very still. There was nothing left for him to say, and no way left for him to say it.

———

The shotgun slammed against Ellie's shoulder. She steadied herself and held the shotgun in the crook of her left arm. She reached up with her right hand to push a strand of hair out of her face. Then she just stood where she was for a minute, smelling the burned powder that drifted in the air and looking at what was left of Jink.

Jonathan walked over and looked down at the body. "That one of 'em?" he said.

Ellie joined him. Jink's face in profile was virtually untouched by the shot except for two places on his cheek.

"That's one of them," she said. "He was the second one."

"Well, looks like you don't have to worry about him anymore," Jonathan said.

"No," Ellie said. "I don't guess I do."

Maybe that should have made her feel better about herself or about Burt, but it didn't. It didn't make her feel much of anything, unless it was a little angry and ashamed of herself for what she'd done.

"Don't fret about it," Jonathan said. "He deserved it."

"Maybe he did," Ellie said. "But that doesn't make it any easier."

"You didn't have much of a choice," Jonathan said. "He was gonna shoot you. He would've done it if he could."

"That's just it. I'm not sure that he could. He didn't do so well with you."

"I was just lucky, or he was just unlucky. He was tryin' hard enough."

"You weren't, though," Ellie said. "Were you?"

Jonathan didn't look up from the body, didn't meet her eyes. "I don't know what you mean."

"Yes, you do." Ellie's face was stiff with anger, but her anger was directed at Jonathan rather than herself. "You were just standing there, waiting for one of those bullets. You didn't even try to shoot. You *wanted* that man to kill you."

"I shot at him," Jonathan said. "You must've heard me shootin'."

"I heard the shots, all right, but I don't think you were shooting *at* him." Ellie brushed her hand across her eyes. "I think you were just trying to get him to shoot at *you*. Even at the end there you were calling him, trying to get him to turn around and shoot at you again."

"Well, I sure didn't want him shootin' at you."

"I'm sure that's true. You wanted him to shoot you." Ellie turned and started to walk away.

"Wait," Jonathan said.

Ellie turned back. "Well?" she said.

"Maybe you're right. It wasn't anything I planned on when we started, though. The idea just kinda grew on me as we were ridin' along. You can see how it was."

Ellie shook her head. "No. I can't."

Jonathan walked over beside her. "You could if you were in my boots. I haven't said this, but I've been in a lot of pain lately, the kind where it's like some-thing's squeezin' you so hard that it's like to break ever' bone in your body."

"I'm sorry," Ellie said. "I should have thought—"

"It's not the pain I've had," Jonathan said. "I've stood it so far, but today it let up on me for the first time in weeks. I feel a whole hell of a lot better. You'd think that was good, but feelin' better makes me real-ize how much I was hurtin'. It won't be long before the hurtin' comes back. I don't want it to come back."

"Isn't there something they can give you to make the hurting stop?"

"Not anymore. The doc gave me somethin', and it worked for a while. Now it don't work."

"But you seem fine now. You might look a little weak, but you don't seem too sick."

"That won't last," Jonathan said. "I've seen some-thin' like it happen before. It's gonna come back, and it might carry me off right quick. That'd be fine. But it might not. So I thought I'd let that fella over there do the job. Quick and easy."

"You don't seem to me like the kind of man who'd want to do things the easy way," Ellie said.

"I didn't use to be. Things get different when you get old, though."

"You're not old."

"Don't fool yourself, ma'am. I'm just about dead, and that's as old as you can get."

Ellie started walking away from him again. "I'm not going to listen to that kind of talk."

Jonathan trailed after her. "I'll stop it, then. We in't got time to argue anyhow. There's still those two ther fellas we got to find."

Ellie didn't stop to wait for him. "I don't think so. Not me, at least. I think I'll just go on back to Blanco nd let the law take care of things."

Jonathan caught up with her and reached out, taking hold of her arm. "You're gonna leave it up to Shag illman? He's the one that'll be the law in Blanco ow. I don't think you can count on him to do much ood."

Ellie shook off his hand. "Well, what if he doesn't? What good did I do, killing that man back there?"

She thought about the way Jink looked as he lay in the dirt, his right side torn away. She had made him ook almost like Burt had, but there was no feeling of atisfaction in having done it.

"Well," Jonathan said, "for one thing he won't be illin' anybody else's husband or rapin' any more women. You can't say that about the one that's runnin' oose."

"I don't care. I don't want to go after him."

"I do."

"Why? So you can try to get yourself killed again? Well, you can do it without me. I'm going back to Blanco."

"You can do that if you want to. You want me to ell you why you ought not to?"

"I don't think you can."

"Well, let me try." Jonathan pushed his hat back

on his head. "Look at it this way. There's two of thos
robbers still on the loose. One of 'em's maybe no
quite as bad as the other'n, but if we don't stop 'em
nobody else will. Shag Tillman sure won't."

Ellie knew he was right. She thought again abou
the way she'd felt in the wagon bed. For herself, i
didn't matter any longer. She had back what sh
needed, and killing one of the men who'd taken it ha
not made her feel any better. It had made her fee
worse, if anything. But what about some other woman
Ellie had learned self-sufficiency early in life. Woul
another woman be the same way? And even if she was
why should that man have a chance at her?

"If we went after him," she said, "would you try t
get yourself killed again?"

"No," Jonathan said.

"You'll have to promise."

Jonathan grinned. "I promise."

"All right, then. We'll go on."

"It's the right thing to do," Jonathan said. "Thi
time, I'll help you." *If I last that long*, he thought
"Now, we better see if we can find that fella's horse
You never can tell. We might be needin' it."

Ellie looked back to where Jink lay. He was noth
ing more than a darker shadow on the ground now.

"Should we . . . do anything for him?" she said

"I don't think there's much of anything we car
do," Jonathan said. "He wouldn't appreciate it, any
how."

"No," Ellie said. "I don't guess he would."

Ben was a little confused about directions, but he thought he was headed the right way. He was really tired, though, and the wound was beginning to pain him considerably. He was beginning to wonder if he was going to make it back to where Jink was. Damn that O'Grady for taking the horse.

A few thick clouds had come up from somewhere, and occasionally they obscured the moon, making Ben's progress even slower. He had stumbled and fallen once, opening the wound slightly and making it bleed again.

With every step, he cursed O'Grady and Gerald Crossland. At least Gerald Crossland was dead. There was a bit of pleasure in that part of it.

Ben judged that it was a little after midnight, though he couldn't be sure, when he heard a horse whicker, a sound that was answered by another horse.

He smiled in spite of himself.

One horse might have been Jink's, but two meant that there was someone else around.

He didn't know who was out here in this godforsaken country with him, but he welcomed whoever it was. They would soon be providing him with a horse and whatever else they had that he wanted.

He thought for a moment about who it could be. Lawmen? That was a possibility. They'd have to be mighty good trackers, and it looked like they would have caught up to him sooner if they were that good.

He thought about the dead marshal. Maybe some-

one had found the body and come looking. Again
that meant they'd have to be fast and good.

Well, it didn't matter. Law or not, they didn't appear to be expecting company, and they were about to
get it.

Ben had reloaded his pistol earlier, and he slipped
it out of its holster. He didn't want to rush things.
He'd just sidle up to the camp on the side away from
the horses. No need to stir things up and announce
that he was coming in. He'd take it nice and easy.
Give the folks a little surprise.

He looked up at the moon. It was sinking now,
and there was a large cloud not far from its face, being
pushed slowly along by the night breeze. He'd get as
close as he could, then wait for the cloud to cover the
moon.

He wondered again who might be in the camp. He
hoped they'd have some water for him.

Chapter 19

---◆━◆━◆---

Ellie couldn't sleep. She knew why, of course. She couldn't stop thinking about the man she'd killed, about the way the buckshot had torn him apart, about the way he'd fallen, like a used-up old rag doll dropped by a child that no longer cared about it.

She'd done exactly what Burt set out to do, at least as far as that one man was concerned, and she wished she could be happier about it. She knew, however, that her motives were in the long run no better than Burt's had been.

And now she had Jonathan Crossland to deal with. He wanted to keep on after the other two men, but he wasn't in the least like Burt. Maybe he'd weakened there for a while and given in to a selfish motive, but when you got right down to it, he wasn't being selfish any longer.

Well, not entirely.

She was sure that he had a lingering desire to recapture something of the man he'd been years ago, but she was equally sure that he wouldn't try again to get himself killed to spare himself the pain he was anticipating. He'd promised about that, and he was the kind of man who'd keep a promise.

No, he wanted to go on for exactly the reason he'd given. Not because it was what people expected of him. Nothing like that. He wanted to go on because it was the right thing to do. There weren't many men like that left. Rawls Dawson had been one, she thought, but she couldn't think of anyone else, not even Burt.

A horse snorted and stamped the ground. Ellie wondered if something was bothering them. Maybe it was only that there was a strange horse with them, the one that had belonged to the man she'd killed. They had found it not far from where she'd shot him, patiently waiting for someone to come and claim him.

She had surprised herself by recognizing him. It was the same horse the man had been riding the day before, but she hadn't even thought about the horses since that time.

It had occurred to her then that she would probably never forget anything about that day. It was one thing to reclaim for herself something of her integrity and self-respect, but it was another to forget what had happened.

Jonathan was right. They had to go on. The other man had to be stopped.

The horse snorted again and Ellie half raised herself from the ground, pushing back the blanket that she had used to cover herself.

The moon was lowering, and a cloud was about to glide across it, but the night was still suffused with a silvery light. Ellie looked in the direction of the horses, but she could not see anything that could be disturbing them. Far off in the distance beyond the horses two owls called, and the long mournful notes trailed off into silence.

Then she heard a muffled sound from the opposite direction. It sounded like something scuffing the dirt, as if someone might be moving quietly up on the camp. She could see no one, but she and Jonathan had laid out their bedrolls near a clump of cedars and oaks. There could be someone prowling there in the shadows cast by the trees.

"Jonathan," she whispered. "Jonathan, did you hear anything?"

There was no answer. Jonathan did not move.

She had shoved the blanket aside and started to get up when Ben stepped out of the shadows, pointing his pistol at her.

"Well, well," he said, recognizing Ellie as quickly as she recognized him. "Can't get enough of it, huh? Had to come looking for more."

Ben knew better than that. He had a pretty good idea why she had come. He was watching her warily.

Ellie had taken off the pistol and hung it on her saddle, but she had laid the shotgun on the ground beside her, and her fingers groped for it.

"No use looking for a gun," Ben said. "I'd kill you before you got to it, and that still wouldn't stop me from doin' anything I wanted to. Hell, you weren't much more fun than a dead woman, anyhow."

Ellie's eyes widened. She could hardly believe what she was hearing. "You're crazy," she said.

"Maybe I am, at that," Ben said. Her comment didn't appear to anger him. He glanced over to where Jonathan lay, unmoving. "Who's your friend?"

"No one you'd know," Ellie said.

"It ain't Jink, is it? He oughta be around here somewhere. You liked old Jink, too, but I'd sure be surprised if he was up to havin' another go at you."

"Jink," Ellie said. "So that was his name."

"Won't do you no good to know it now."

"No, I guess not." She wasn't going to tell him what had happened to Jink.

Ben walked over to Jonathan and prodded him with the toe of his boot. Jonathan still did not move.

"Heavy sleeper, ain't he?" Ben said.

"He was sick," Ellie said, feeling a sudden sadness sweep over her. "He might be dead."

"Looks like it, sure enough." Ben prodded Jonathan again, and when he didn't move, Ben looked at Ellie and smiled. "I guess he won't be botherin' us any."

"You're hurt," Ellie said, noticing the wound for the first time.

"Don't worry. It won't slow me down none. You treat me right, and I might let you live."

Ellie didn't believe him, and it didn't matter even if he was telling the truth. She was not going to treat him right, no matter what.

But he didn't have to know that. "I'll treat you right," she said.

Ben walked over to where she sat. He kicked the shotgun out of the way.

"I know you will," he said, slapping her so hard that her head twisted until her chin hit her shoulder. She fell backward to the ground, unable to move.

Jonathan was not dead. He was asleep and dreaming.

The day's ride, the brief flurry of action, both had tired him much more than he had realized, and he drifted off to sleep nearly as soon as his head touched the saddle that he was using as a pillow.

It was a deep and healthy sleep, very much unlike the ragged dozes of the last weeks, the kind of sleep generally enjoyed only by cats and babies.

No slight noise, no nudge of a boot was going to waken him from a sleep so calm and deep.

In his dreams he rode the prairies with the great cattle herds once again. He was young and strong, smelling the dust of the trail, the scent of hundreds of cows mingled with his own sweat. He felt the stickiness of his sweated shirt sticking to him, heard the creak of his leather rigging and the bawling of the moving cattle.

If he had died then, in the midst of that dream, he would have died happy.

But he didn't die.

Ben kept the gun in one hand and undid his belt buckle with the other. To hell with O'Grady. Ben was going to have himself a little fun. There were plenty of horses here. He'd take them and catch up with O'Grady later.

The woman lay there waiting for him. He squatted down and reached to throw her dress up over her face.

When he did, her fist came up from the ground and smashed into his wounded shoulder.

It was as if someone had stuck a red-hot knife in his shoulder and twisted it.

"God *damn!*" he screamed, dropping his pistol and sitting back on his haunches.

Ellie attacked him like a wildcat, punching her fist into the wound with one hand and clawing at his face with the other. She felt his skin tear under her fingers and she tried to gouge out his eyes.

"Jesus Christ!" Ben yelled, throwing up his good arm in an attempt to protect his face.

He fell backward and Ellie fell on top of him, hitting and clawing.

Pain was making Ben weak, but it was also making him desperate. He was so much bigger than Ellie that he was able to sit up even with her on top of him, and when he managed to get in a blow to her face, he knocked her back and away from him.

She twisted around and came at him again, but this time he was ready. He doubled his fist and hit her hard on the point of the chin. Her head snapped back, and she fell.

"Bitch," he said. He got shakily to his feet and aimed a kick at her head.

Ellie grabbed his boot in both hands as it came at her head and twisted hard to the right. Ben fell, landing on his wounded arm.

"Oh, Jesus!" he said.

Ellie sprawled across him, sinking her teeth into his shoulder as near to the wound as she could get.

Ben yowled like a dying dog.

Ellie bit down harder, trying to make her teeth meet through the hunk of skin and muscle that she had clamped down on. With one hand, she gouged the wound in Ben's shoulder. With the other, she beat at Ben's face. She felt something crunch under her fist, and she hoped it was his nose.

Ben howled louder.

Ellie kept on biting and hitting. There was a roaring in her ears like the roaring of the wind in tall cedar trees on a stormy night.

She was dimly aware of something touching her back, of some sound other than the roaring, but she ignored it until Ben at last stopped screaming. Even then she didn't stop hitting and gouging and biting until someone took her by the shoulders and shook her, shook her hard.

"You can let up on him now," Jonathan said. "I think he's passed out."

The muscles of her mouth seemed frozen, but finally she was able to open it and let go. She sat up and spit into the dirt several times. The she wiped her mouth with her dress.

"Too bad we don't have any likker," Jonathan said. "Might be good to wash your mouth out about now."

She looked at him. Her eyes were filled with tears. "Why didn't you wake up? I thought you were dead."

"Dead to the world, more like it. Best sleepin' I've done in a month of Sundays. But you might know nobody'd let me enjoy it."

Ellie brushed at her eyes and attempted a smile. "I'm sorry I bothered you," she said.

Jonathan kicked Ben with his toe. "Looks like you didn't have much of a choice. Sorry I wasn't much of a help to you, but by the time I woke up I couldn't shoot him. Too much chance of hittin' you. And by the time I got over here, you didn't look like you needed my help. Don't look like I've done you much good on this whole trip we've been on."

Ellie stood up. "I'm glad you came."

"Me too. It's been a good many years since I've seen a fight like that one. Fact is, I don't think I've ever seen one quite like it. Never with a woman in it, anyhow."

"He was going to—"

"I know what he was goin' to do. Looks like he won't be tryin' it again anytime soon, though."

"Is he dead?"

"You sound like you'd be sorry if he was."

"I would. Is he?"

Jonathan knelt down and felt Ben's throat. "He ain't dead, worse luck. What're we gonna do with him?"

"Take him back to Blanco," Ellie said.

When Ben regained consciousness, his arm was hurting him something fierce. He jerked his head and tried to sit up, but his hands were tied in front of him with a strong lariat and he made a clumsy job of it.

"Glad to see you decided to join us," Jonathan said. "My name is Crossland. I think you knew my boy."

"Yeah, I knew the fat bastard," Ben said.

His face was hurting him, and he knew his nose was broken. He thought there was blood in his mouth. He spit on the ground. Blood, all right.

"You killed him," Jonathan said.

"He needed it," Ben said, twisting his head to wipe his mouth on his shirt. That hurt him, too.

He looked at Jonathan suspiciously. "You was supposed to be the next thing to dead."

"I am," Jonathan said. "You would be, too, but the lady here didn't want me to kill you."

Ben turned his head to look at Ellie. He started to say something, but the look in her eyes changed his mind.

"What're you gonna do with me?" he said.

"Take you back to Blanco," Ellie told him. "Let you stand trial for what you did."

Knowing that he was in no immediate danger restored a bit of Ben's confidence. Jink was around here somewhere, and if the little bastard hadn't died, he might be able to help Ben out.

"Be hard to prove I did anything," he said.

"Not so very hard," Ellie said. "I can testify to one thing, and Mr. Crossland can testify to the others."

"What others?" Ben said.

"You killed the marshal after you killed my boy," Jonathan said. "I saw you."

"The hell you did."

Ben turned his head and looked around. Jink must surely be around here somewhere. Why didn't he show up and do something? It would be just like the sorry little rat to have died.

"If you're lookin' for your pard, you don't have far to look," Jonathan said. "He's not gonna be much help to you, though."

"Damn," Ben said. "Where'd you find him?"

"He found us," Ellie said.

"Worse luck for him," Jonathan said. "There ain't much left of him to pray over."

Ellie turned her face away at that, and Ben said, "You killed him?"

"That we did," Jonathan said. "But he was going to kill us if we didn't. You, now, I'd just as soon kill you where you're sittin', but Miz Taine don't think that'd be a good idea for some reason or another."

Ellie turned back to them. "Get up," she said.

Ben wasn't sure he wanted to get up. He didn't move.

"Maybe you're right, Jonathan," Ellie said. "Maybe he'll just be too much trouble to us. Go ahead and kill him."

"Wait a minute, wait a minute," Ben said, scrambling to his feet. It wasn't easy with his hands tied, but he did it.

"Now let's go over here and get you on this horse," Jonathan said. "It's your pard's horse, but he won't be needin' it no more."

They had to help Ben mount. It was an awkward process, but he was able to put his tied hands around the saddle horn and get aboard.

"While we're ridin', I reckon you can tell us about the other man that was ridin' with you," Jonathan said.

"That Irish son of a bitch," Ben said.

"I'd watch my language if I was you," Jonathan said.

Chapter 20

Shag Tillman was up before sunrise, waiting at the little Blanco jail for the arrival of the Texas Ranger. He didn't know what time the Ranger would arrive, and he'd gotten up at the first rooster crow so he could be at the jail waiting. He didn't want anyone to think he was getting lazy now that Rawls Dawson was no longer there to look over his shoulder.

The telegram he'd received night before, not long after delivering Dawson's body to Fowler's, had said there would be only one Ranger coming. Shag hoped that one Ranger would be enough. He wouldn't much want to go chasing after those three killers all by himself, and he would be surprised if the Ranger did, either.

If the Ranger did want to go out after them, Shag hoped the Ranger wouldn't ask him to go along. He had to stay there in Blanco, after all. He told himself that it was his job to protect the town now that Rawls

Dawson was gone, and he didn't see how he could very well go traipsing off after anybody, even if they were robbers and killers, and leave the town without a lawman in case of emergency.

He looked out at the streets to be sure there wasn't an emergency occurring right that very minute.

There wasn't.

There was hardly anyone stirring in Blanco at that time of the morning. Mr. Rogers hadn't opened the mercantile store yet, and there was no one over at the White Dog Saloon except old Hodge Mason, who swamped the place out every morning in return for a drink or two later in the day. There was a mangy cur dog wandering down the street, looking for something to eat or maybe a cat to chase. He didn't find either one.

Shag went into the jail and brought out a sturdy wooden chair. He put it near the wall and then sat down in it, shifting his weight until he was comfortable.

He had just tilted back to watch the sun change the color of the sky from gray to blue when a movement at the corner of his eye attracted his attention.

He sat up, the chair's front legs thudding against the boards of the narrow porch floor that ran in front of the jail. Someone was coming into town from the west.

Shag couldn't make out who it was. It was too dark back in that direction to see much, but he could tell there was more than one of them. Couldn't be the

Ranger, then. He wondered who'd be riding into town so early. He hoped it didn't mean trouble, not that he couldn't handle it, but he'd always had Rawls Dawson to tell him what to do in the past.

He had it in mind to ask for Dawson's job, and he didn't want to make a misstep right off and maybe turn the town against him before he got a chance to prove he could handle the marshal's job on his own.

On the other hand, maybe this was his chance to show what he could do. If there was some kind of trouble coming, he could go right out there and put a stop to it.

That idea didn't appeal to Shag at all.

He had to do something, though, whether it was dangerous or not, so he went around to the side of the building where his horse was tied and got in the saddle. He'd just ride out to see who was coming in. There shouldn't be any harm or danger in that. He hoped.

By the time he got to the edge of town, the riders were close enough to identify. It was old Jonathan Crossland and Ellie Taine, and they had a man with them, a rough-looking man that Shag didn't recognize. The man was riding his horse, but Jonathan Crossland was holding the reins, leading the animal along.

Shag couldn't quite figure out what Miz Taine was doing with Jonathan, but if he was to believe the note that had been pinned to Rawls Dawson's vest, the man with them must be one of the robbers who'd killed the marshal.

The man sure didn't look much like a dangerous outlaw now, slumped in the saddle the way he was, and Shag wondered if there was some way he could take advantage of the situation, maybe get some of the credit. That was the kind of thing that would make him look good in town.

He hailed the riders. "Howdy, Mr. Crossland, Miz Taine. Who's that y'all got with you?"

"This here's one of the killers that robbed our bank," Jonathan said. "We're bringin' him in."

Shag heard the "we." "You mean Miz Taine—"

"Yep," Jonathan said. "She went with me. We got another one of 'em too, but he's still out where he fell. You don't have to be in any rush to send after him."

Damnation, Shag thought. That wasn't goin' to look too good. An old, dying man and a woman had gone out and tracked down the robbers while he sat on his butt and waited on the Rangers to arrive in town.

"Well," he said, "I surely do appreciate you bringin' him in. I guess I can take over now. We got a nice little cell just waitin' for him down at the jail."

He looked at Ben, who sat quietly, still slouching in the saddle, his wrists bound, his crossed hands resting on the saddle horn.

"He looks about half dead," Shag said. "Must've give you a little bit of a fight."

"Not much of one," Ellie said.

Shag didn't know exactly what to make of that. "We'll just see that he don't do any more fightin' for a long time," he said.

Jonathan was reluctant to hand over the prisoner, but Shag was the law. He was about to pass Tillman the reins when Ben went into action.

Ben had been docile for the entire ride, but only because he was waiting for the right opportunity. It looked like this was the only one he was going to get.

He jerked upright and kicked his heels as hard as he could into his horse's sides. The animal jumped forward, smashing into Jonathan Crossland's mount and spilling the old man into the dirt.

Jonathan's horse shied sideways into Shag's mare. She danced back, and while Shag tried to bring her under control, Ben's horse raced forward.

Ben knew that surprise was the only thing he had going for him, that and the fact that the damn woman was too soft-hearted to shoot him. If she'd wanted him dead, she'd have let the old man kill him last night.

If he could get through the town without being stopped, he could get away again. He was sure of it. His hands were tied, but he could still ride. He could take care of his hands easily enough when he had a little time to himself.

He felt a tingling in his veins, and he knew he was going to make it. He knew it just like he knew that sooner or later he was going to find O'Grady and get his share of the money. No woman could stop him, not even with the help of some sick old man, and no half-witted lawman could stop him, either.

He was still thinking that way when he heard the boom of the Navy Colt behind him.

Surprised, he turned his head to see the woman, still astride her horse but lifting herself in the stirrups, holding the big pistol in both hands and firing in his direction.

"God damn," he said. He was scared, but the bullet didn't come anywhere close.

The pistol boomed again.

"God damn," Ben said again, bending low over the saddle. "She just won't quit."

He didn't say anything the next time. He didn't have a chance. The .36 caliber bullet struck him in the lower back, hitting his spine and straightening him up in the saddle before it ricocheted off the hard bone.

The next bullet hit him about a foot higher, almost in the middle of the back, where it glanced off his rib cage and entered his heart. The heart ruptured instantly, and Ben fell to the left and out of the saddle.

But he didn't leave his mount entirely. His bound wrists hung on the saddle horn. The horse kept on running, Ben dangling on the side, his boots dragging twin trails through the dirt of Blanco's main street.

Shag had his horse under control now, and he sat watching, open-mouthed. *God a'mighty*, he thought. He'd never seen anything quite like it.

Ellie fired again.

"You can stop that now," Shag said, figuring she was out of bullets anyhow. "I think you got him. We better see about Mr. Crossland."

Ellie lowered the pistol slowly. There was nothing in her face except concern for Jonathan.

Shag had dismounted and was kneeling by the old man.

"Is he all right?" Ellie said.

"I don't think so," Shag said.

The Ranger was a man named Paul Utley, and he was about as big a man as Shag Tillman had ever seen, well over six feet tall, and wide enough for his shadow to darken a barn door if he stood close by. He had on a leather vest, with a shiny silver badge pinned to it. The badge had been handmade from some kind of big silver coin.

Shag had just finished telling Utley the story of the past day and night as best he could piece it together from what he'd been told by Ellie Taine. She was in a hurry, and she hadn't ever explained why she was with Crossland. Shag didn't see that it mattered much, anyhow. What mattered was that the Ranger got the gist of the story and didn't think that Shag had been neglectful of his duties.

"So what you're telling me is that this old man and this woman brought one of the bank robbers into town and killed him when he tried to make a getaway. And they killed another one and left him out there somewhere," Utley said, gesturing with his thumb toward the open door.

They were sitting in the jail, Shag behind the marshal's desk, Utley front. They had to sit. Utley was nearly too tall to stand in the low-ceilinged room, at least with his high-crowned hat on.

"That's right," Shag said. "That's exactly right."

"And these robbers killed the old man's son and the marshal of this town, not to mention the woman's husband and a teller at the bank."

"Yes, sir. That's what they did."

"And there's one of them still on the loose."

Shag nodded. He hated to own up to it, but that was right, too.

"You goin' out after him?" he said.

"Yes. But I expect that he's a long time gone by now."

Shag wondered if there was an implied criticism in Utley's tone, but he couldn't detect it if it was there.

He decided he'd better say something anyway. "We went out after 'em, but their tracks was washed out by the rain. Marshal Dawson said so."

"I'm sure he was right," Utley said. "Nevertheless, I'll see what I can do."

"You don't seem in much of a hurry," Shag said.

And that was a fact. The Ranger had arrived around the middle of the morning, and he'd taken his good time in getting around to talking to Shag and hearing the straight of the story. He'd talked to Mr. Wiley at the bank first, and then to old man Whistler.

"No need to get in a rush," Utley said. "He's got too much of a start for that. Anyway, your marshal, the one that got killed, was a good man. He sent a description of the three men in his telegram, and if

I've got this story right, the only one of them left is a red-headed Irishman."

"As best we can tell," Shag said.

"Well, then, I'd say that his best chance of crossing the border would be down around Laredo. We've got a Ranger station there, and if he comes anywhere near, we'll get him."

There was a quiet confidence in the Ranger's voice that Shag envied. He believed every word that the Ranger said.

"I just bet you will," he said.

"And just for good measure, I'll be going along behind him," Utley said. "I'm not a betting man, myself, but if I were, I wouldn't give good odds on his chances."

Shag nodded. "Me neither."

"I'm glad you're in agreement. Now, suppose you tell me more about this old man and the woman who caught up with the other two."

Shag was glad to get onto another subject before the Ranger could ask him to come along after O'Grady, and he eagerly launched into the story of Jonathan Crossland's illness and the death of Burt Taine.

The doctor hadn't wanted to allow Jonathan Crossland to return home, but Ellie had insisted, so the doctor, with the help of some of the onlookers who had gathered at the sound of the shooting, loaded Jonathan into the doctor's wagon. Ellie followed them to the ranch on horseback.

It was cool and quiet in Jonathan's room now. The doctor had gone back to town, telling Ellie that there was nothing more that he could do.

"I don't know why he's lived this long," the doctor said. "It's a wonder he didn't just fall out of the saddle and die when he first got on a horse. If I didn't see the evidence of it, I wouldn't believe he'd ridden half a mile, much less done what you've told me."

"He did it," Ellie said.

"There's no need for you to stay," the doctor said. "He has a cook who comes in. There's nothing you can do."

"I'll stay," Ellie said.

She sat there now, in a hard wooden chair beside Jonathan's bed, watching the old man sleep, wondering if he would ever wake up again. It didn't seem fair to her, somehow, the way things had turned out.

Jonathan had seemed just fine on the ride back to town, maybe even better than he had the day before. She had almost convinced herself that he would be all right, though he'd told her more than once that he wouldn't.

"Wishin' for it won't make it so," he said at one point. "I've wished for a good many things in my life, but I don't think I ever got a one of 'em just because of the wish. I had to do somethin' or other ever' single time, and this time there's not a thing I can do."

Nevertheless, he had seemed fine, talking, laughing, even trying to josh their prisoner, who just slumped on the horse and never said a thing.

His sullenness was all just pretense, Ellie saw now. He'd managed to kill Jonathan in the end, just by knocking him off his horse, or that was the way it seemed.

Ellie knew it wasn't really that way at all. A little fall like that wouldn't have bothered a healthy man a bit. So it wasn't the fall. It was whatever had been wrong all along.

She looked at Jonathan again. She hoped that he'd wake up one more time. There was something she wanted to tell him.

It was midafternoon before he stirred. At first Ellie thought he was only dreaming, but after a minute he opened his eyes and looked around the room.

"Home," he said.

"Yes," Ellie said. "You're home. How do you feel?"

Jonathan tried to sit up. Pain twisted his face, but he pushed himself up and leaned back against the headboard.

He rested a minute, and then said, "I've felt better."

"Would you like some water?"

"Now that's a fine idea, if you wouldn't mind pouring it for me."

Ellie took a pitcher off the stand by his bed and poured the water into a cup. She handed it to Jonathan, who took it in both hands to steady it. He put the cup to his lips and drank the water.

"I wanted to thank you," Ellie said as he drank. "For going with me."

"Glad to do it," he said, handing Ellie the empty cup. "I wasn't much help, but I had me a pretty good time." He looked around the room. "The doc been here?"

"Yes," Ellie said.

"Bet he was surprised to hear about our little trip." Ellie smiled. "He was."

"Figgered. I don't expect he thought he'd ever see me again until he saw me in a pine box."

"Don't talk like that," Ellie said.

"Just a little joke," Jonathan said. "I wish he'd stuck around for a while, though. Somethin' I got to do."

There was a knock on the front door.

"I'll go," Ellie said.

"I thank you. Whoever it is, you bring 'em in here. And I'd appreciate it right much if you could go in the other room over there and bring me a piece of paper and a pencil."

Ellie didn't know what he wanted paper for, but she said, "Of course. Let me get the door first."

The man filled the doorway. "I'm Paul Utley," he said. "Texas Rangers. Are you Mrs. Taine?"

Ellie told him that she was.

Utley took off his hat. "I wonder if I could talk to you and Mr. Crossland a minute."

"He's very weak," Ellie said.

"I won't take long."

Ellie led him to the bedroom, stopping off for a piece of paper and a pencil on the way. Then she introduced Utley.

"Pleased to meet you," Jonathan said. "Sorry I can't get up to shake your hand."

Utley laughed and leaned down, extending his hand. "I'm pleased to shake with you any way I can."

"I guess you wanta hear about those two outlaws," Jonathan said.

"That's right," Utley said. "If you don't mind."

"I don't mind," Jonathan said.

After Jonathan was finished, Utley thought for a second. "Thieves fall out, you think?"

"Sure enough," Jonathan said. The effort of talking had tired him, but he had shushed Ellie when she tried to stop him. "The one we brought in was wounded, and we sure didn't shoot him. Must've been the other partner."

"Who's still out there."

"Dead or alive, one or the other," Jonathan said. "I'd say alive, since the one we brought in didn't have the money, and neither did the other one we met up with."

"But the third one could be wounded as well," Utley said.

"Could be."

"Well, I appreciate your telling me all this. I'm

sure we'll get the third one. I'll go now and leave you alone."

"I wish you'd stay a minute," Jonathan said. "There's somethin' I'm of a mind to do, and I need a favor."

"What's that?" Utley said.

"I want to write a new will," Jonathan said.

Jonathan Crossland died in his sleep that night.

Ellie was beside the bed all night, and she never closed her eyes, but he slipped so quietly from life to death that she never knew when the moment occurred. His skin was cool to the touch when she took his hand in the early morning light that came through the window, so she knew it had been some time earlier, maybe as much as an hour.

She crossed his arms on his chest and pulled the blanket up to his chin. Then she stood looking down at him. Tears welled in her eyes, but she brushed them away. There was no need for tears. Jonathan Crossland had gotten what he wanted, a day and a night of freedom from the pain. And now he would be free of it forever.

The enormity of what he had done for her the previous afternoon was still at the forefront of her mind. She only hoped that she was up to the challenge.

"I can't take it," she said when he told her what he was going to do.

"Yes, you can, and it's all legal. Couldn't ask for a better witness to a last will and testament than a Texas Ranger."

"If I take it, I can't handle it," Ellie said.

"Shoot," Jonathan said. "A woman that can hunt down the men that killed her husband, and you say you can't handle a little old ranch? I grant you it won't be easy. I'm not gonna give you the money. It's already promised to them orphans."

Ellie had finally given in. "I'll do my best," she said.

"I know that," Jonathan said. It was just about the last thing he'd said to her.

She looked down at his face and smoothed his brow with a work-hardened hand.

"I'll do my best," she said again.

O'Grady looked out over the muddy Rio Grande. It was flat and smooth and sluggish. The sun glinted off its surface, and O'Grady could see a sandbar about halfway across.

He leaned over and patted his horse's neck. "Well, old fella, looks like we made it."

The horse was drinking from the river and made no response. The other horse, the one O'Grady had taken from Ben, was drinking as well.

O'Grady had not gone to Laredo. He'd thought about it, but he was worried about the Ranger station there. You never knew what that small-town marshal might have done. He might have alerted all the law in the state.

So O'Grady had gone farther west, toward Eagle Pass and Piedras Negras. He could cross the river a long way from Laredo and work his way back down to the border town if he wanted to. He didn't think he would, though. He thought he'd head toward Monterey.

He hefted the money sack. He had enough there to last him a long, long time. Maybe he'd have to spend the rest of his life south of the border, but he might not have to take any more risks. He could buy a little store or maybe a cantina. It was worth a try.

He thought for a minute about Ben. There had been a time or two earlier in the day when O'Grady had thought there might be someone on his trail, away back. There was nothing special he could point to. It was just a feeling he had.

It didn't matter now, though. Once he was across that river, everything would be different.

The horses were through drinking, and O'Grady urged them forward. He knew that he might never return to Texas again, but he didn't mind. He didn't even look back.

Epilogue

+‑+ ≡◆≡ +‑+

It had been a hard few months for Ellie Taine. She had buried Jonathan Crossland under the cottonwood tree beside his son, but with more dignity than Gerald had received. And then she had gone to the bank for a loan.

The Blanco bank hadn't been able to accommodate her because of the robbery. She'd had to go all the way to San Antonio, and the banker that she talked to there had at first been wary of letting a woman have any money. After she'd proved to him that she was indeed the owner of a considerable property that could stand as security, however, he'd seen things differently.

And the ranch was going to pay for itself. There wasn't much question of that. Ellie had Juana to help her in the house, and she'd hired a couple of hands who could wrangle the cattle, do the roping and branding of the calves when the time came, and keep up the fences. Things were going to work out just fine

Or they were if people would just leave her alone.

At first she didn't understand why they kept coming to her, but then she realized that the story of what he and Jonathan had done had gotten around, and that it had grown in the telling. People thought she was some kind of female gunslinger, or even something more than that, someone who could set things right when they'd gone badly wrong.

Shag Tillman had been one of the first to come asking for her help. Not two weeks after he'd been made town marshal, someone had broken into Alf Rogers' mercantile store.

"Now that our bank's been robbed, they prob'ly think they can just walk in here and carry off the whole town," Shag told Ellie.

"Who's 'they'?" Ellie wanted to know.

She was standing on the porch of what she still thought of as Jonathan's house, looking up at Shag, who was sitting on his horse under a hard blue sky. The wind stirred up dust devils that danced across the yard.

"They's whoever it is that broke into Alf's store," Shag said.

"What did they take?"

"Just some coffee and vittles, nothin' much."

"Maybe it was just somebody who was hungry. You can find them if you try."

Ellie could say it, but she didn't really believe it. She wasn't sure Shag would be able to find his hat if

someone were to take it off his head and hang it on
peg somewhere.

"I could sure use a little help," Shag said, and Elli
could tell it was a hard thing for him to admit.

"I'd like to help you Shag," she said. "But I jus
don't have the time. I've got a ranch to run now, and
can't be doing your job for you."

That had made Shag mad, and he rode back int
town without saying another word to her. But h
wasn't the last of them.

There was a woman whose son had run away
mainly, Ellie surmised, because of his father's casua
brutality. She didn't think it would do any good t
look for him, and she figured he might very well b
better off wherever he'd gone. So she told the woma
that.

The woman had left crying, which had made Elli
feel terrible and had even caused her to be out of sort
with Juana later that day.

Why won't people just leave me alone? she won
dered.

But they didn't. They kept coming, and she kep
turning them away. They had troubles, but she ha
troubles, too. Running the ranch wasn't easy. Hov
could they expect her to leave it to help them out o
their difficulties?

One day she went out to Jonathan's grave, ou
under the cottonwoods away from the house and awa
from anyone who might ride up seeking her help.

She looked out over the green of the pasture an

istened to the breeze rustling the thick leaves of the cottonwoods. It was a peaceful place to be, a place where she could think about things and try to get them straight in her mind.

"Do you think they'll forget about what we did?" she said, looking down at the spot where Jonathan lay.

She wasn't expecting an answer, and she didn't get one.

"After all," she went on, "it wasn't much. We didn't even bring the money back."

The breeze stirred the hair on the back of her neck, and she smoothed it with her hand. It didn't seem to make any difference about the money. People didn't care about that, if they even thought about it. By now, they probably thought Ellie *had* brought the money back. A man last week told her he'd heard about how she'd faced down a gang of outlaws and shot three of them before they could even draw their guns. The story just kept on getting bigger, and people just kept on coming by.

Sooner or later there might even be someone that Ellie would want to help, maybe some woman who'd suffered the same thing that Ellie had, or even something worse.

"What am I going to do then?" Ellie said.

She didn't get an answer that time, either.

I'm not the law, she thought, *and revenge isn't all it's cracked up to be*.

Nobody would believe that last part, even if she told them, which she never had. And while she wasn't the law, she could probably do a sight better at the job than Shag Tillman, though she would never say that to anyone.

She believed it, however. She'd proved it to herself, and to Jonathan. Not to mention the men who'd raped her.

She sighed. She had a hollow feeling in her stomach, and the feeling told her that someday there would come an appeal she couldn't deny, an appeal that would take her back into the kind of violence she didn't want to face again.

But not today. She had other things to do today. She took one more look at Jonathan's grave, then turned and went back to the house, to whatever was waiting for her there.